ADELAIDE'S FATE

G. BAILEY

BOOK ONE

CONTENTS

Other Books by G. Bailey   vii

Description   xi

Prologue   1

Chapter 1   7

Chapter 2   23

Chapter 3   34

Chapter 4   44

Chapter 5   56

Chapter 6   63

Chapter 7   71

Chapter 8   78

Chapter 9   84

Chapter 10   93

Chapter 11   105

Chapter 12   112

Chapter 13   118

Chapter 14   129

Chapter 15   137

Chapter 16   151

Chapter 17   158

Chapter 18   166

Chapter 19   173

Chapter 20   180

Chapter 21   187

Chapter 22   193

Chapter 23   199

Chapter 24   204
Epilogue   209
About the Author   213

PART ONE
BONUS READ OF HER WOLVES

Description   217
Chapter 1   221
Chapter 2   232
Chapter 3   242
Chapter 4   251
Chapter 5   257

Spring Court

Autumn Court

Summer Court

Winter Court

the land of

FRAYAN

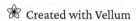 Created with Vellum

MORE BOOKS BY G. BAILEY

HER GUARDIANS SERIES

HER FATE SERIES

PROTECTED BY DRAGONS SERIES

LOST TIME ACADEMY SERIES

THE DEMON ACADEMY SERIES

DARK ANGEL ACADEMY SERIES

SHADOWBORN ACADEMY SERIES

DARK FAE PARANORMAL PRISON SERIES

SAVED BY PIRATES SERIES

THE MARKED SERIES

HOLLY OAK ACADEMY SERIES

THE ALPHA BROTHERS SERIES

A DEMON'S FALL SERIES

THE FAMILIAR EMPIRE SERIES

FROM THE STARS SERIES

THE FOREST PACK SERIES

THE SECRET GODS PRISON SERIES

THE REJECTED MATE SERIES

FALL MOUNTAIN SHIFTERS SERIES

ROYAL REAPERS ACADEMY SERIES

THE EVERLASTING CURSE SERIES

THE MOON ALPHA SERIES

For all those who love stormy nights.

DESCRIPTION

How far can fate make you fall?

When Adelaide turned twenty, losing her parents and gaining custody of her fifteen-year-old sister were not part of her plan.

If being a shifter in a world where her kind is hunted wasn't bad enough, she now has to protect her sister too. Adie has no choice but to move into the old house her parents left them, or risk being on the streets in a dangerous world.

Only she didn't expect to be living next door to a strange, and very attractive, group of men who are far more than human.

They offer her protection in exchange for keeping their reason for hiding from the humans a secret and helping them. But protection comes at a cost, and the cost is something none of them could have expected.

A cost that's been destined. A cost that fate has weaved for Adelaide. A cost that even princes cannot escape.

(Her Guardians series spin-off)

PROLOGUE

"Run faster," the breathless voice of my mate's best friend shouts to me as I rush through the cold woods in Scotland where we planned to escape to. At least our information on the portal was right. The freezing wind hits my face as snow brushes against my bare legs, making me want to fall into the snow and give up. I fight the cold, unforgiving snow for as long as I can. Keeping the image of my mate in my mind. He would never give up.

"I can't," I say, collapsing to the ground as pain rips through my stomach. I look down as blood coats the snow-covered floor by my stomach. I can't do this anymore, it's too late, and I can feel the poison spreading through my body from the dagger.

"Reni," I whisper my companion's name as she slides to her knees in front of me, my gaze goes to my newborn daughter that she holds in blankets close to her chest. Two hours, that's all I had with her before they attacked us. *It's not enough.*

"I will stay and fight to protect you, for him," Reni says sharply, handing me my daughter, and I push her away gently, my heart breaking as she cries.

"No, go. It's too late, and I can't outrun them. I can distract them enough by closing the last portal," I say quietly as Reni's eyes widen in shock. If I close that portal, then there is no way for her and her army to follow us.

"Using any power now will kill you. My alpha died to keep you alive. You can't do this to me," she begs me, keeping her voice in a whisper for the baby. I look around the snow-covered forest, remembering the Autumn court and the brief happiness I felt there when I married the man I loved and had my beautiful daughter. The Autumn court was always home and where I expected I would die one day. Now I'm going to die in Winter, on Earth, of all worlds. So very far from home.

"Something is wrong, and neither of us are healers. Take my child and keep her safe. Please," I say reaching to hold a hand against my sleeping child wrapped in her arms. I twirl a finger around the dark red hair on her head, the same colour as mine and all the royal family before me. Her bright green eyes watch me, and she doesn't make a sound. She is so innocent for the world she has been born into. Reni looks down at me and then to my little baby she holds in her arms.

"I will do it for you. I will do it for my lost alpha and my queen. I will bring her up with my mate as our own. No one will know who she is," Reni says, finally giving in, and I know her well enough to know she means every word. She may not be Fray, but she is family to me.

"Her name is Adelaide, after my mother," I tell Reni gently, who nods.

"That name will give her identity away on Frayan," Reni reminds me what I already know. It is a royal Frayan name. No common Fray could name their child it. It would be highly disrespectful. Not that it matters. Once she stepped into Fray, everything about her would give her identity away.

"No one can know who she is. You must keep her away from anything Fray-touched. She must never get her Fray powers or wings," I tell her, knowing that there is no way she can be taken back to Frayan. When I close the portal, it will be impossible, but there are weapons here that have Fray magic, even some creatures that have passed through portals. They won't have enough magic to reveal her powers, but over time...they would make them appear.

"You have my word. I'm sorry I can't save you," she says with tears running down her face. Everything starts going blurry as she stands and offers me a hand to help me up. I stand shakily and look down once more at Adelaide before turning away, my heart breaking. *I have to do this.*

"They are coming, go," I say, and she nods holding my daughter closer.

"I'm sorry," she bows the best she can when holding a baby. My mind flashes back to the prophecy surrounding my child and the Fray courts that have fallen to keep her safe. She has to be safe. I watch until I can't see Reni anymore before walking back off into the woods. When I see the portal, a slightly blue clear shimmer that only Fray can see, I lift my hands. It only takes a second for my light-ening power to shoot purple bolts of lightning out my hands into the portal. My wings flutter behind me, lifting me slightly into the air as my power gets stronger. The portal cracks slowly, bit by bit until it explodes, and I go flying into the air. I close my eyes and think only of Adelaide, knowing she will be safe, as darkness takes me.

CHAPTER
ONE

"Adie, why do we have to move? The old house was fine," my little sister says as she groans from her seat next to me in my small car. The car that somehow seems smaller every time she asks me the same question. *Shitadoodle, what do I tell her?* I look over at Sophie, who is sat with one ear plug in and doesn't take her eyes off her tablet as she waits for an answer I don't want to give her. I can't worry my fifteen-year-old sister with the facts about our money situation, and the fact we have absolutely none. The truth of the matter is that our parents liked to travel around all the time, and that wasn't good for keeping a long-term job. All the traveling meant that when they died two months ago, in a car crash, I had to sell our house to pay off our debts and then move my sister into the house left in the will. I look out at the snow and ice on the road, deciding I'm not going to like this small town. Well it's not that bad, as Scotland isn't too far away and remote. The new house is only seven hours' drive away from York, where I was at university. *Deep breath, and answer her, Adelaide.*

"Adie," Sophie sighs louder than before, and I put my foot on the gas a little more and pray my piece of crap car will actually get us to the house. God knows I don't have the money to pay for a pickup truck or any idea who to call. The old Peugeot is traveling way too far than I would have ever trusted it to, but I really can't afford to pay for a new car.

"We are nearly there," I finally say. That was a lame answer, and I know it.

"Great," she huffs, and I just catch her rolling her eyes at me from under her brown hair before she goes back to whatever game she is playing on her tablet.

"I know this is a big change, but it will be good for us," I tell her as she finally looks at me for a second before huffing in response, again, and going back on her tablet. Sophie used to be a chatty twelve-year-old who loved sports. Or at least that's what I remember her being like when I left for university, but now she is a shell of herself since our parents' death. My heart drops as I remember that they are really gone, and I have a teenager to look after, with no job and hardly any money. I haven't had time to grieve because I can't melt down in front of Sophie. It's going to be difficult enough to find work that works around Sophie in a small town. A university dropout isn't a good person to hire. I had no choice but to leave when the accident happened; I couldn't move Sophie into my shared dorm at university with what the world is like now. *They would kill her and me for one slip-up.* The small village finally comes into view after over an hour of driving down an empty country lane. The village is near enough to a big town, so I can drive there to work in the day, and it apparently has a very good school that I've gotten Sophie into. She doesn't start for a few weeks though, and considering we can hardly talk to each other, the idea of being stuck in an old house for weeks is not appealing.

It takes me a few wrong turns down empty roads until I find a row of four houses. Our house is the last of the attached houses, and it has its own driveway that I pull up in. Sophie finally looks up from her iPad and frowns at the sight of the overgrown lawn and old paint falling off the outside of the old house. *Home, sweet, home.* The house looks close to falling apart, and it takes everything in me not to slam my head against the steering wheel at the sight. The estate agent said it was in good order, this isn't what I thought it would be like. I wrench my door open, muttering "fuck" to myself as I slam it shut behind me and go up the two steps to the door. Thankfully the locks look new, kind of, and the door opens easily before I walk in.

The smell of dust is the first thing that hits me as I look around at the hallway, which has cobwebs in every corner, and it is empty of any decorations. The space isn't too bad I guess, and it is painted in a light brown which matches the wooden floors. There are three dark wooden doors, one at the end and one on each side of the hall. I open the first one to a small empty room which I'm guessing is a storage closet or study. The next room is a lounge with a large fireplace, two covered sofas, and a small coffee table. This room isn't too bad. I go to the window and open the thick cream curtains, coughing from the dust and pushing the window open to let some air in here. I pull the white sheets off both sofas, and they are brown like the colour all the rooms have been painted in, by the looks of it so far.

I leave the lounge and go to the door at the end of corridor, opening it up to find a kitchen. The kitchen is a similar brown to the walls, with dark wooden counters, and I thank god when I see there's a working fridge and cooker that just need plugging in. After a little moving things around, nearly dying from inhaling more dust, I manage to get them turned on. I open the window in the kitchen, letting some more much needed air in. I am going to be up all night cleaning this house from dust and cobwebs. When I come back to the door to get some boxes, Sophie is walking up the stairs, and shouts down from the top, just as I grab the handle.

"The beds don't look bad. Bring me some of my stuff up, won't you?" she shouts, and I groan internally while pulling the door open and shuffling my feet back to the car. When did she get so damn bossy? Can I even tell her off for it after we lost mum and dad? I'm no parent to her. Sophie and I have never been the closest of sisters. We argue more than get along, but now everything has changed, and I don't know where I stand with her. I shake my head, knowing I can't overthink this, and I need to just take one day at a time. I'm so lost in my thoughts, that I don't look where I am going at all. The next thing I know, I trip over what I assume is a large rock in the middle of the driveway and brace myself for the hard fall I'm going to suffer. Somehow that doesn't happen; instead, I feel a warm chest against my back and strong big arms wrapped around my stomach as someone catches me. I turn my head to thank whoever it is, and my breath catches. The hottest guy I've ever seen is staring at me with sparking clear blue eyes. His dark brown hair is short on the sides with an overgrown fringe which has blond tips, and he has a five o'clock shadow. I have to blink a few times to find out if he is real, because men don't look like this. No, only gods do, I imagine.

"I don't usually have girls fall for me without knowing their name," he says, a casual smirk on his lips as I stare speechless at him. *They don't make men like this in Britain, or anywhere, so where the hell did he come from?* I reluctantly pull out of his arms and move to stand in front of him. He is really tall, as I have to stretch my neck to look up to see his face. I'm not that short, but this guy must be well over six foot.

"I'm Adie," I hold out a hand, and he slides his slightly cold hand into mine. The man gives me a slight, deep sexy chuckle as he turns my hand over in his before pulling it up to his lips for a gentle kiss.

The moment his lips touch my skin, I feel a shock, that's the only way to explain it, and by his widened eyes, I know he feels it too. I pull my hand away quickly, and my body takes a step back before I even realise it. I don't know what the hell that was, but my hand is still somewhat tingling from the contact.

"It is nice to meet you, Adie. I'm Rick. My brother and I live there," he points to the house next door to mine, "with our two friends." I internally sigh at the fact I have to live next to the hottie who no doubt knows his way around women, and I know I will be drooling over him for the considerable future. Not that a guy like this would be interested in me. I have hips, no boobs to be seen anywhere, and I'm a twenty-year-old virgin. I'm way out of my league with this guy. Not that it matters. The last thing I need right now is any distractions from looking after Sophie. Holy hotness, this means I have to live next to four guys who might all be as hot as this dude, and somehow keep focused. I can only hope they mow the lawn shirtless once in a while. *That would be awesome to see.*

"Adie, where are you? If you are going to take this long, I'll get my own stuff," Sophie's unimpressed voice comes from the door, and I turn to see her just stop when she sees I'm talking to someone. Her eyes watch Rick carefully, and I have to clear my throat to get her attention and to stop her from doing something crazy like be territorial and growl at the human guy.

"This is my sister, Sophie. Sophie, this is one of our new neighbours, Rick," I introduce them as Sophie walks over to us, stopping at my side. Rick holds a hand out to Sophie, who looks at the hand in disgust before ignoring him completely by going around us to the car.

"I'm sorry about her," I say as my cheeks go red at Sophie's behaviour. I watch her open the boot and start pulling out boxes, putting them down as she looks for her bag.

"No problem. I know what it is like to be an angry kid. Do you want some help with the boxes?" Rick asks me, and I glance up at him. He is smiling, no sign of him being angry or not understanding, and in fact, there is sympathy etched across his features.

"If you're not busy," I find myself replying, even though it is dangerous to make friends with any humans when we need to be invisible in this village. Though he hasn't noticed how my teenage sister is lifting very heavy boxes out of the boot like they are pillows, so we might be okay. I can just let him help with the boxes and then make an excuse so he has to leave. Nice and simple.

"Nope. It's my day off work, and I literally have nothing to do," he tells me with a big grin. I laugh as he goes to the car just as Sophie walks past with her large backpack, flashing Rick a glare which he thankfully ignores. Part of me wants to tell her off for being rude, but her eyes look watery, and so much has changed for her that I can't help but feel sorry for her. This can't be easy. I pat her shoulder as she goes by, and she nudges me away in clear anger. I swallow the hurt as I watch her run into the house before I go to grab a box. I get to the back of the car just as Rick picks up three boxes like they weigh nothing. The boxes have kitchen written on the side of them, so I know they are filled with heavy plates and kitchen things. I don't say anything as I follow Rick in with my one box. I could have grabbed three or more like he did, but that might give away my secret, and my parents taught me better than that growing up. Learning to pretend how to be human is something built into my bones at this point. It's Sophie I worry about. There were several times we had to run and leave everything because she forgot how deadly it is for humans to know what we are.

"Wow, you must work out," I say as we put the

boxes on the floor in the kitchen, and I carry one of them into the lounge.

"Sometimes," he mutters behind me, and I look back to see him watching me strangely or something, before leaving the house for more boxes, I guess. I forget the look, following him out after putting my box down, and together we get them all in the house with little trouble.

"Thanks for all your help, can I ask where the local store is?" I ask, noting that it's getting dark, and I need to get some food for Sophie and me to eat tonight. "Actually, don't worry, I will just Google it."

"The store closes soon, so it's pointless to go now. I will order pizza. The pizza shop is literally five minutes away, and I'm a regular," he winks at me, and then pulls his phone out, calling for pizza without waiting for my reply.

"Ah thanks. A takeout would be good for the first night," I say, grabbing my bag off one of the boxes in the lounge. Rick follows me in, chatting on the phone to the pizza man like they are best friends.

"Put the money away, it's on me. Any preferred toppings?" he asks, and I shake my head, putting my purse back. Judging from his slightly demanding tone, he isn't going to let me pay.

"Surprise me," I reply, my voice more husky than

usual, and I swiftly realise that I'm flirting. I quickly look away, reminding myself that this man is a human and out of my league. *Jesus, control yourself, Adie.* It's been like an hour, and I'm already flirting and forgetting everything my parents told me. *Get it together, Adie, you can't flirt with humans anyway. Wolves and humans don't date, everyone knows that.*

I leave him to order and take a box of Sophie's stuff up the stairs. It's a pretty basic house with a small bathroom in the middle and two rooms on either side, which is just like the photos of the house in the will. But the photos made it look much nicer than it is. I follow the only light on to the room on the left, the one Sophie must have claimed. The door is slightly open, so I can see that Sophie is sat on a chair in the one room with her iPad and doesn't notice me come in. I place the box on the floor by the door, looking around the simple room. There is a double bed with a mattress, and Sophie has made up her bed with her purple sheets. The wardrobe is open, and she has even started to put clothes away before getting bored I suspect. I'm just glad it isn't that dusty in here.

"Soph, Rick is ordering pizza. Will you come and eat with us?" I ask gently, and she finally looks up at me. I see straight away that she has been crying, and it's heartbreaking to see her like this. I walk over and pull her into a hug even as she protests by trying to push me away. "You don't have to be strong around me. I miss them too. I'm sad too, and there is no one that understands what you are feeling like I do."

"I miss them so much," she cries, relaxing into my hug as I look down at her iPad and the photo of mum and dad on it. They are both smiling in front of a tent, with Sophie right in the middle of them, a big goofy grin on her face and one tooth missing because she fell out of a tree the day before, knocking it out. Luckily, it was only a baby tooth that hadn't fallen out yet. I remember taking this photo years ago when we went camping. Like we did every year because it was the only safe place to shift and run together as a pack. It doesn't even seem real that they are gone, and we will never get to do that again. I hold Sophie tighter to me, so grateful that at least she is alive and didn't get into the car that night. If I had lost her as well...I can't even imagine losing her.

"I miss them more than I could ever describe, but I want you to know I'm here. You always have a home with me. I'm not mum or dad, and I'm crap at knowing what is best, but I am going to try my best to make this work," I tell her firmly, because I mean every word.

"Thanks, Adie. You're the best sister. I'm sorry I'm a little shit at times," she sniffles.

"Mum would threaten to wash your mouth out with soap if she heard you say 'shit'," I joke, and it seems to lighten the mood as she smiles at me.

"I know, but she said 'shit' a lot. Just usually under her breath when she dropped something or was mad at dad, but she would usually add 'head' to that one," Sophie says, and we both laugh as she pulls away. It hurts to look at Sophie sometimes because she looks so much like mum, her brown hair is the same dark colour, and she has her brown eyes too. It just reminds me how much I do not look like my sister or my parents.

"So, pizza?" I ask, reminding myself why I came up here in the first place and that Rick is waiting downstairs.

"Sure. Call me down when it gets here, please," she replies.

I kiss the side of Sophie's head before walking out of her room and pause in the hallway, staring at the full length mirror that is half covered up by a blanket. I pull the blanket off and stare at myself for a second. In some ways, it is good that I don't look like Sophie or my mum because I don't remind myself of mum. Mum was willowy thin, with thin brown hair and dark brown eyes. Dad was similar looking, but in a more geeky way when mum was more delicate. I twirl a bit of my dark red hair around my finger, which is thick and wavy down to my waist. My hair isn't a tiny bit thin, it is thick and uncontrollable at the best of times. My bright green eyes shine back at me, the green complements my shiny red hair. Whereas my parents had dark tanned skin like Sophie, mine is pale, and no matter how much I sun tan, it sure doesn't change. My hips make my shirt rise a little, revealing a little bit of skin, and I pull my shirt down to cover it. I know I shouldn't have eaten that second chocolate muffin at the garage we stopped at, but at the time, I didn't feel a tiny bit guilty. I think back to the conversation I had with my mum once about why I look so much different than them, and I asked if I was adopted or something as a joke. Mum just snapped that I looked like her brother and then left the room like her ass was on fire. I always wished I had asked her more, and for pictures of her brother, but it's too late now. I shake my head, stepping back and hanging the sheet over the railing on the stairs. I know it's just moving into this new home and losing my parents that is making me feel like this. I just need to relax for a bit. I run down the stairs, walking into the lounge.

"Everything ok?" Rick asks me from where he is sat on the sofa, looking comfy with his feet on the coffee table.

"Yeah. I don't know if Sophie will come down, but she might do," I reply, feeling awkward. "It's been a rough few months, and she is only fifteen. I know she is sorry about earlier."

"Is she your sister?" he asks with clear questions in his eyes. He must be wondering how a twenty-year-old, or however old he thinks I am, is looking after a fifteen-year-old alone.

"Yes. Our parents passed away a few months ago," I say quietly as my voice still catches as I admit it.

"I'm sorry, I know what it's like to lose your mother, but mine was when I was a lot younger. I have a stepmum anyway, so I was lucky. Hell, I'm not making this any better, am I?" he asks me, rapidly speaking like he is nervous, and we both chuckle.

"Then I'm sorry about your loss too," I comment, and he nods.

"So...what brings you to Midview village, i.e. the

land of the boring old people," he asks, leaning back and grinning at me. Whatever nervousness he had is lost, and he's back to being charming, which is somehow making me nervous.

"My parents owned this house and not much else. I thought it would be a good place to start," I say, and he nods.

"Our reasons are similar apparently. We all needed a new start too, and this place had the perfect job. At least for now," he says, and then suddenly goes serious as he leans forward, placing his hands on his knees.

"When were you going to tell me that you're a shifter? And while you're at it, why the hell are you really here?"

TWO

My heart must be banging a million miles a minute as I watch Rick's eyes glow like mine in the dimly lit room. A growl escapes my lips as he finally stops hiding his wolf, and its presence overwhelms mine—he is powerful. *An alpha. How did he hide?*

"How did you appear so human to me?" I ask, my words coming out as more of a growl as my wolf pushes me to shift and challenge Rick in order to protect Sophie. Rick stands up, and I do the same, keeping still and refusing to back down. I hold his gaze, knowing it is never smart to run from a wolf. Let alone an alpha wolf. Though I've never run from my own kind before, it's just what my mum always told me.

"A gift of mine, but I won't hurt you," he says moving closer to me, holding his hands up, and I can't feel any kind of threat coming from him. I don't know if he is telling me the truth, but when he takes another step closer, I let out a long growl, and I almost let my wolf take over. He does pause though, not pushing me any further, which surprises me a little, but my growl must have caused Sophie to panic, as the next thing I see is a brown bundle slam into Rick's chest. It knocks him over, and he hits the sofa as he falls. I rush to pull Sophie off him, but a long growl from Rick stops me. He slowly stands up, holding Sophie as she tries to bite him and claw at his shirt, ripping it in places.

"Sophie," I plead as Rick picks her up by the scruff on her neck, holding her away from him, and she whines in annoyance.

"That was unexpected," Rick grunts, looking down at his shirt. "I loved this damn shirt, pup."

"Don't hurt her," I beg, moving slowly closer to them as panic fills me until I can't stop shaking. I'm a little shocked when Rick softly places Sophie into my arms. Sophie licks my chin as I look down at her, checking she is okay even though I know she is.

"You shouldn't attack an alpha, pup," Rick laughs, and his big hand strokes her head. I'm surprised when she happily lets him fuss her. "I used to challenge my uncle when I was a pup, until I learnt it wasn't a good idea until I got older and stood at least a little bit of a chance."

"I've never met another wolf, other than our parents. Neither has Sophie, and our parents were not alphas," I tell him, and he frowns briefly, going to say something, but a door slams open, and a man walks in the open lounge doorway. The man smells human, but everything from the way he stands to the way he stares at me like he is planning my death tells me he is anything but. Sophie whines as I place her behind me on the sofa and move in front of her with a growl at the man whose gaze darkens. The man has wavy black hair that curls away from his face, revealing his dark blue eyes. They are so dark, you can only just see the blue, and without staring like I did, you would think they were just black. The man keeps his hands at his side, tightly in fists, and his muscular arms press against his black leather jacket.

"What the fuck is going on, Rick?" he asks in a deadly calm voice, which is somehow seductive. It sounds like a voice that could talk you into dying for him without saying much more than a whisper. Even though he asks Rick the question, his eyes still watch my every move. Assessing everything about me, I bet. I run my eyes over him, having the feeling he is not a wolf, he seems too deadly for that. Everything about him sends shivers and warning bells through me, yet I can't seem to pull my gaze away.

"Josh, we have new neighbours. Two wolves who have no pack and are clearly in hiding," Rick says, maneuvering himself so he is in front of me and cutting my gaze from Josh off. I move to the side, not wanting to be blocked, and Josh only smirks at the action.

"Then send them to the castle before anyone notices," Josh retorts. "*She* needs to fucking leave."

"I'm not going anywhere, but why don't you get the hell out of my house before I make you," I suggest, crossing my arms and keeping my head high. "Get out."

"You have no idea who you are taking to, sweetheart," the man growls, a light blue shimmer appearing all over his skin as he reveals the massive black wings on his back. *Angel. A dark one.* I growl low until Rick moves in front of me, blocking my view of Josh again.

"Leave, Josh. I will figure out who they are, but I don't sense a threat here. You need to calm the fuck down," Rick warns, a low growl slipping out with his words. "Calm it down now or we need to take this outside, and I don't want to fight you again, bro."

"I am calm, brother," Josh replies smoothly, though his gravelly voice suggests otherwise.

"Josh..." Rick warns him again, this time his words are filled with an alpha demand. It's enough to make me shiver and want to fall to my knees in submission, but I fight it off. *I won't submit to anyone.* I glance back at Sophie, whose wolf has submitted in a heartbeat and is rolled onto her back, showing her stomach off. It would usually make me chuckle, if it were in a different circumstance, that is.

"Fine," Josh responds, and I glance around Rick just in time to see Josh walk out the door, leaving it open behind him. The sound of the front door opening and shutting is heard not long after. There's an awkward silence as Rick turns around, lifting a massive, muscular arm and rubbing the back of his head.

"You might want to stay away from Josh...he won't hurt you, but he doesn't like strangers. Especially not right now," Rick says, defending his brother.

"Got it. Stay away from tall, dark and downright terrifying is something I can do," I mutter and turn around, picking Sophie up. I walk her to the stairs and place her on the bottom one. "Run to your room and change back. We are safe, I just need to talk to Rick alone." Sophie whines, pressing her head against my hand before running up the stairs like I asked her to.

"Why are you here?" Rick asks me, and I turn around to see him leaning against the door frame like a model for a magazine. I go to answer when the front door bell rings, and Rick goes to answer it. I can smell the pizza from here, without even opening the door.

"Go and sit, it's the pizza," he tells me, holding the door handle as I pause, not knowing if I can trust him. "I promise that I will never hurt you. I only want to talk and understand why you are here without a pack." I don't answer him, but I do walk into the lounge and awkwardly sit on the sofa. Rick comes back in the room not long after and slides the pizza on the coffee table, opening it up.

"I would get plates, but everything is in boxes," I say, reaching across and breaking a piece off as Rick sits on the other sofa with his own piece.

"You don't need plates for pizza," Rick says, shrugging his massive shoulders, and I agree. We eat silently, to the point that it is seriously uncomfortable.

"What do you want to know?" I ask when I have finished my slice, and Rick has already finished his and had a second one as he eats super quickly. He spreads his arms back across the top of the sofas and watches me closely.

"Where is your pack?" he asks. "What is their name, and why are they not protecting two young females?"

"We don't have a pack. My mum and dad said there were no packs around anymore, none that could be trusted anyways. We kept moving to keep safe," I explain, and he looks confused as he processes my answer for a few seconds.

"That's not true, Red," Rick mutters. "There are plenty of packs that protect their own, and until ten years ago, they were spread all around the world."

"I don't know why my parents didn't go to any, but they always kept us hidden and moving around. What happened in Paris...well we had to keep super low down after that," I say, referring to how Paris suddenly had a massive ward appear all around it for months. When the ward came down, most of the people in Paris were missing or dead. And some of the people had turned into things almost like zombies. It soon came out that supernaturals were real and had caused what happened in Paris. After that, anything different or suspected as supernatural was hunted and usually killed. Everywhere in the world suddenly became extremely dangerous overnight for people like my family.

"Coming here is not keeping you safe. You need protection, an alpha and a pack," Rick mutters angrily. "Your parents risked your life way too much by hiding you."

"Why? We have done fine without one. My parents clearly kept us alive and fine," I remark, folding my arms in annoyance, and he huffs, shaking his head.

"The world is dangerous for supernaturals. Hunters are everywhere and actively hunting anyone different," he tells me what I already know.

"I know that. We are good at hiding, and this village is tiny, no one will look for us here," I retort. It's not like I moved into the middle of London where I couldn't shift and would be found super easily.

"This village is not what it seems. You need to leave," Rick says gently, but it is firm and a demand.

"We have nowhere to go. I had to drop out of university, I have no job, and this house was all that was left in my parents' will," I admit to him. "I couldn't sell this house if I tried, and I have to do what is best for Sophie."

"Shit," Rick grumbles, rubbing his face. "Then I guess I will look after you for a week. We have a place I can get you to, and you will be safe. You will be with your own kind."

"There is nowhere safe," I remark, not understanding where he thinks I can just go to.

"I grew up in the safest place for supernaturals, and my stepmum is the queen of the supernaturals. Winter will give you both a home and protect you. She does that for anyone that needs help," he explains to me. I stare at him for a second in shock. There is a queen of the supernaturals and somewhere safe to live? Sounds like a fairy tale. If Rick's stepmum is queen, then he must be a prince. Just my luck to trip over and literally be caught by Prince Charming.

"I don't know..." I let my voice drift off.

"I'm not living here for no reason, and this village is more dangerous than anywhere else. Let me help you," he asks. "I want to help you."

"Now I think about it, I've heard rumours of the supernaturals having a queen and four kings. That they hide all the supernaturals with them. It was a story told around university," I reply, being honest with him. "It always sounded like a fairy tale that couldn't be true. My parents said it must be lies, and I really didn't think on it until now."

"Not one part of it is a lie. I am prince, heir to the supernatural throne, and I promise on my blood to protect you," he says, and goose bumps spread all over my skin as we stare at each other. "You are my pack, and as your alpha now, I will keep you safe no matter what." The more I stare at Rick, I get the feeling he isn't joking one bit, and what he did was very serious.

"Rick, look, how can I believe you?" I ask, standing up and resisting the urge to pace as I keep eye contact with him. I won't drop my gaze, not when I know he is an alpha, and my wolf wouldn't let me anyway. I've never been a submissive wolf. My parents once submitted to me when I was mad about something silly. I just didn't know I was an alpha female until then. Mum and dad said alpha wolves are rare and meant to be more powerful than usual wolves. They are meant to lead. The only place I would lead anyone is into trouble, so that can't be true.

"That's the thing, you already do trust me, but you don't know *why* you trust me," he says, grinning as he stands up and walks to the door. "Come over to our house and meet the others in the morning. They will want to meet you, and we need to sort out a way to make you seem human."

"Are they as scary as Josh?" I ask quietly, not wanting to touch the subject about how I trust this hottie already. I'm sure it's just a wolf thing and nothing to do with how damn sexy, protective and stunning he is. Rick laughs, and I resist the urge to shiver at how nice his laugh sounds.

"No one is as scary as Josh," he winks at me, and walks out the room. I wait for the front door to shut before collapsing back on the sofa, not having a clue if I am right for trusting the handsome next door neighbour. *Or if I just made a big mistake.*

CHAPTER
THREE

"At least the wolf neighbour bought pizza," Sophie comments, sitting on the sofa with the box and practically inhaling it all as I pace near the old brown fireplace. I shake my head and go to the window, shutting it before closing the curtains, which are still a little too dusty for my liking. Once I find the vacuum in one of the boxes, I can sort that out. I look back at Sophie, wondering if it would be worth asking her if she knows anything.

"Did mum and dad ever say anything about other packs? About a castle and a queen of the supernaturals?" I ask Sophie, trying to make my tone gentle, like I am asking about an everyday thing as I open one of the boxes and take out the red blanket. Though I'm pretty sure I fail at it because my voice comes out high pitched. I suck at this.

"Nope," Sophie says slowly, her tone quiet. I stop, glancing at her as she puts the pizza box down and hurries to get up. "I'm going to my room, I was just hungry."

"Night then," I reply, as she smiles at me before walking out of the room as quickly as she can. I watch her go, knowing she might be lying to me or just wanting to avoid talking about our parents. *Who knows?* After putting the blanket on the sofa, I pick the pizza box up and take it into the kitchen, turning the light on and sliding it on the side. I look around at the wooden counters, the island with stools in the middle, and I notice it must have been cleaned recently but just not well enough. I open the cupboards and am relieved to see someone has wiped them down, and there is some washing up liquid left in the cupboard by the sink. At least the estate agent brought a cleaner in like I paid them to do. I grab the box with the kitchen things in and put all the things away before pouring myself a glass of water and walking out of the room.

I pause next to the boxes, seeing the small one

on top that is all we have left from our parents. It was left in the will, but I haven't had a chance to open it because planning the funeral, leaving university and packing up the old house took up too much time. Or I just haven't wanted to open it yet because part of me is scared what might be inside it. I lock the front door, before picking the box up and going up the stairs. I pass by Sophie's room, but the door is firmly shut, and I doubt she wants to see me anyway. I know there are only two bedrooms, and I walk to the third door, opening it up and switching the light on. There is a plain wooden bed with a sheet-covered mattress on top, a dresser and a matching wardrobe. The window in this room is small, but it lets in moonlight through the thin white curtains. I shut my door behind me and kick off my flat shoes, before resting the glass of water on the dresser. I take the box to the bed with me and sit down, crossing my legs as I look down at the box. I know I need to open it to see what my parents left. Mum and dad always knew there was a chance they could die. We are shifters in a world that wants all supernaturals destroyed, so it's logical they left important things in a will.

I shake my head and tell myself I need to open the damn box and get it out of the way. I pull the

Sellotape back, opening it up to see two letters in envelopes and one tiny ancient looking jewellery box. I pick one letter up which has 'Sophie' written on it. I put it to the side and pick up the other one, which has my name written. I run my finger over my mum's handwriting, trying to hold in any tears, knowing I have to be brave and open it. I open the letter rapidly, knowing it's like ripping a Band-Aid off. It's better to do it quickly. God, I need some chocolate ice cream or a muffin. Or anything at this point that is high in calories and I will regret the next day. A trip to the shop is the plan for tomorrow, before meeting the other neighbours. The letter is written on flower covered paper that I remember my mum always using to write anything on. When I was a kid, I used to love to borrow some to draw on. Pretending to be like mum was a fun game. I swear she had an unlimited collection of this flower paper because she never said no to sharing it with me. I take a deep breath for courage before I start to read the note.

My sweet Adelaide,

First off, I love you. Please remember that always as you

read this. I love you so much, and so does your dad who is sat here watching me write this. You might not understand all this, but know that loving you was something that was true throughout all the lies. It's the only thing I feel like I told you the truth about. I do not know how to explain everything in one letter, but I must try because, if you are reading this, death has found me. I was not born on Earth, and neither were you. There is a world called Frayan, and it is attached to Earth like many other worlds. Frayan is the land of the Fray or fairies, as humans know them. There are many names for the people and creatures I used to live with. Two days after you were born, my beloved alpha, a wolf fate, died saving his people and queen. I had grown up with him, he was like a father to me. I would have died to save him, if I were given the chance, but his death was so swift, no one could have prevented it.

He left behind a heavily pregnant mate.

I am bound to tell you no more, but I know you need answers. I knew one day you would ask the questions without me saying a word. That one day your true powers will reveal themselves, or worse, she will find you and tell you a twisted version of the truth before killing you.

I planned ahead in this event, and in the attic of the home we have left you is those answers.

In the box is something left to me by my alpha...your father.

Please wear it. It belongs only to you now.

I cannot tell you of your mother, oh I wish I could. I wish so many things that I feel like you will learn in the most painful ways. Life is not fair to you, and oh how I wish I could change it, my sweet Adelaide.

They both would have been so proud of the young woman you have grown into.

The answers lie in the attic, though it might take you a while to figure it out. The Fray make promises, and those promises are woven in powerful magic...remember this.

I promised never to tell you who you are...it was the only way I could keep you safe all these years. I am sorry I cannot say more.

Protect Sophie please, and never let her know this. She is your sister, just not in blood, but I hope that means little now.

This is your secret to bare, and your past to find.

Remember, I love you. Remember to never trust anyone, especially not anyone who is different like you. Trust must be earnt and promised. Fray make promises, child.

Never go to Frayan. Things worse than death wait for you there, my sweet Adelaide. So many have died so you can be here. Do not let that go to waste.

Live.

Love.

Be free.

And please don't hate us for never telling you.

Love you always. Mum and Dad.

I DROP the letter on the bed, my shaking hands just hovering where I was holding it as I repeat several parts of the letter over and over in my head. Mum and dad were not my real parents. I wasn't born on Earth. Someone wants me dead, and there are so many unanswered questions in this letter that I will never be able to ask anyone about. Until a tear drops onto my hand, I don't notice how completely frozen still I was. They weren't my biological parents. I repeat the same thing again and again. My biological father is dead, and god knows what happened with my mum. I suppose she is dead as well, or why wouldn't she come back for me? It takes me a few seconds to realise I'm the reason they have run from packs, from everything all these years. They didn't want anyone to know how different I am and risk me getting found. The way mum speaks about my biological father, it is clear she thought him as pack. Mum and dad left everything behind to save me. I can't process how my father was dead before I was born, and I have no clue who my mother was.

I stare down at the letter, reading the last line again. *Love you always. Mum and Dad.* Despite this, they were my parents. Mum and dad were always there for me, always loved me, and that must have been real because they never made me feel like I wasn't their child. I had a lovely life growing up, even moving around all the time. This letter changes nothing about that. I take a deep breath and lower my shaky hands to the box, holding the edges as I calm myself down. No matter my birth, my parents loved me. I know that I'm more upset they never told me all this, but if magic stopped them, how could I blame them for that? Mum said she did it to protect me...but protect me from who? Where the hell is Frayan? I shake my head, knowing that I won't get those answers by sitting here.

I wipe my tears away before picking up the small box. I open the lid, revealing a bracelet. It is made of gold with three red gemstones in the middle. The stones glow for a second when I run my finger over them, and I wonder what kind of magic is in these. I glance at the letter for a second, before clipping the bracelet onto my wrist. The stones glow once more when it's clipped, before going back to their ruby red colour. They match my hair, oddly enough. I look back into the box at the last letter. The letter for Sophie. I can't even acknowledge that she isn't my sister by blood, because it means nothing important. Blood is nothing compared to a bond made with love. I wipe my eyes one more time before getting off my bed, walking to the door and opening it. I walk down the corridor to Sophie's room, and knock two times. I wait for a few moments before she opens the door slightly and frowns at me. Sophie has gotten ready for bed, even though it isn't that late, and I wonder if she was napping before I woke her.

"This is for you, from mum and dad's will," I tell her, lifting the letter and showing her before she can say a word. She stares at the letter for a while, before shaking her head.

"I can't read it...not yet. It doesn't feel like they are really gone, and if I read that...it might be true, and I don't know how to cope with it or anything that letter says," she says, her words filled with a heartbreak I understand too well.

"I've just read mine, and you're right. This is going to be hard to read," I admit to her.

"Will you keep it for me?" she asks, and I can only nod before she shuts the door. I stare at the old wooden door for a few seconds, before looking up at the attic door right above me. Tomorrow, I find out whatever is in this house that mum and dad wanted me to find, and tonight I can cry before putting a brave face on and being the woman my parents raised me to be.

"Who is she?" Josh demands, the moment I walk in the door. He is stood in the middle of the corridor, his arms crossed, his black wings spread out as his slightly glowing blue eyes wait for my answer. I bet he has been pacing here since he left Adie's, knowing Josh. I shake my head at him and head to the lounge, and straight to the bar. *I need a drink.* I don't know what happened when I caught Adie in my arms on her driveway, but the need to protect her was overwhelming. There was this almost instant connection, and the only thing I can imagine is that she might be my mate. I can't know for sure until my wolf sees her, but I've never had that kind of reaction to anyone before. I hear Josh following me as I go up to the bar and grab the bottle of Scotch off the counter that someone has left out. I grab two glasses before pouring the drink, hearing Josh tapping his foot behind me.

"Have a drink," I tell Josh and take my own drink to the sofa, sitting on the edge and sipping on it, feeling the burn all down my throat which is damn soothing. What kind of fucked up world is it that my possible mate turns up next door to me when I'm on a mission? I would usually tell Josh, but the way he reacted to Adie, I don't think telling him she might be sticking around in our lives forever is the best idea.

"Who is she?" he demands, watching me closely. Josh and I grew up together after the war, and there hasn't been a day we haven't been in each other's lives. We literally shared a room as my stepmum took him after he lost his dad, and it was the same for Mich and Nath. We made our own pack, made our own rules and never kept secrets from each other until shit went wrong last year. This mission was meant to help us bond, but that never happened, and now I'm not even sure telling Josh this girl might be my mate is a safe idea. Shit, I don't think telling Nath and Mich is smart either. None of us want to fuck up this mission, and she could do just that.

"Adelaide, a shifter. Her and her sister walked into the wrong village, that's all. They aren't anything to do with our mission," I tell him what he wants to know, "though her parents left her that house, and I think you should look into her parents' past and see who they were. Why they would leave a house here for their kids." I might regret asking Josh to look them up, but he is the best with computers, and he can find anything about anyone quicker than anyone I know.

"Freddy—" Josh starts off, picking up his drink and leaning against the bar.

"You know I hate you—or anyone—calling me that," I groan, before downing my drink. Only my stepmum and uncle call me that now, purely because I can't make them stop.

"Shit, old habits," Josh says, downing his own drink and looking at me seriously. "Adelaide is damn dangerous to have here right at this moment."

"I am going to contact my aunt and get her to come take Adelaide and her sister to the castle," I tell him, knowing that is the best thing to do. Even if she isn't my mate, this place isn't safe. If she is my mate, there is no fucking way in hell she is staying around here and risking her life. "I would ask Winter and the others to take them in, but with the baby on the way...I think it's best we don't worry them. If any of them think we have blown this mission, they will pull us back home and all our work is lost."

"That's exactly what I'm worried about," Josh snaps, looking frustrated. "We have been here four months, and we are so damn close."

"My aunt will help, quietly," I say, and shrug my shoulders. "The problem will be solved in a week." I think back to Adie, the moment I caught her in my arms and felt a buzz run over my skin as I looked into her green eyes. She is damn stunning. A woman any man could lose his mind over, and she had to move in next door when we are on a mission. If she was a girl I bumped into back home, it would be a different story.

"Until she goes, we should give her and her sister a protection crystal just in case," Josh grumbles. "I will get Nath to make one for each of them tomorrow."

"She doesn't scent as just a wolf...did you notice anything?" I ask, wondering if Josh could pick something up that I missed.

"I can't see auras, so no. She looked like a typical gorgeous red head to me," he muses, and I refrain the primal urge to beat the shit out of my brother for calling her gorgeous.

"I don't know what she smells of. Even her wolf scent is off. Which is weird considering the amount of half breeds I have met growing up," I say, moving past his statement about Adie. It's not like we haven't shared women before, so I know he wouldn't fight me for her. I don't even know if she likes me back, so I don't know why I am worrying like crazy.

"All the more reason to get her the hell out of here, brother," Josh retorts. "Call and make it happen." I watch as Josh storms out of the room, wondering exactly what is making him more pissed off than usual. He never reveals his powers, and yet he was close to it at Adie's house. Josh doesn't let his wings out often, only defensively, and that is odd on its own. I pull my phone out my pocket and call my aunt, waiting as it rings and rings. The scotch didn't help the feeling in the back of my mind, and I try to think about the last time I had blood to drink. It must have been last Monday. I need a real drink, and it might calm me down a tad.

"Hello, my boy! How are you doing, laddy?" My aunt's thick Scottish accent comes down the phone, and I chuckle before answering her. Hearing her accent always makes me feel at home somehow.

"All good. I need a favour," I say quickly, getting straight to the point, and she sighs.

"I could have been guessing that, Freddy," she replies. "Go on, out with it."

"First off, don't be telling Uncle J or Winter...or dad about this. You know how they overreact," I remark. Dad has a temper when his family is threatened, so does Uncle J, but his wolf has more of a bite, and Winter still treats me like a kid she needs to protect. I love them, but they don't think rationally, and I know they think this mission was too much for us to do so young. Winter and her mates would have done this mission if she weren't pregnant, and I know they are just looking for a reason to pull us out of this.

"They do not overreact, boy. The last time you asked me not to tell them something, we ended up with one burned-down cottage, a wad of humans who were missing their hair, and two random goats. I wish I had told them, now I think back to it," she says, and I cringe, remembering Nath's eighteenth birthday party. That was a good night, just not so much of a good morning when we realised how crazy the night had gone.

"I was a kid, give me a break," I groan, hearing her laugh. *She never lets that story go.* "This is a little more serious."

"Out with it then," she replies more seriously this time.

"Two sisters have moved into the house next to ours. They are shifters, and if anyone notices them, we are screwed," I tell her, leaving out the possible mate part. If I told her that, she would tell Uncle J in a heartbeat and bring us all in.

"Now that is a problem. Have you explained they must leave? Whose pack are they from? Why are they not hidden?" she rapidly asks me.

"That's the problem, they aren't from any pack. Their parents just died recently, and they have nowhere else to go but the house they are in," I tell her, hearing her sympathised sigh before she replies.

"They are lucky to be alive. The hunters—" she starts off, but I cut her off. I can't think of the hunters touching Adie without my wolf stirring and my fangs slowly dropping down. This isn't going to be easy.

"I know. I need you to take them back with you," I ask.

"When?" she asks, agreeing straight away, no hesitation. My family is always there for me. Pack means family, and I was taught you do anything for family.

"Next Monday. We are out on a trip, and it is the only time the house won't be watched. Neither will next door," I say. "I will tell her to be ready for you, but none of us can be there. We have to keep the boss distracted."

"I will make the plan. How old are the sisters?" she asks.

"One is a kid, and the other is about our age, I reckon," I reply.

"A girl looking after a kid at your age...that reminds me of your uncle looking after you as a kid," she mutters, and I hear a deep grumble of a voice in the background. "Is that Freddy?"

"Jaxson wants to talk to you. Speak soon and good luck," she says before there is a rustling as the phone is handed over.

"What is wrong? Why didn't you call me first?" Uncle Jaxson demands, of course thinking something is up without me saying a word. I love Uncle J, but we clash a lot now. I guess it's because we are both alphas, and neither one of us is willing to give up. *Let's just say practice fighting was fun.*

"Nothing is wrong. I wanted to talk to my aunt," I reply.

"Bullshit," he states and chuckles.

"You can't prove it, old man," I joke, and laugh at the line of swear words that he mutters under his breath. *He hates that nickname.*

"Seriously, Freds, is the mission going all good? Anything you need? We can get you out in less than ten minutes if you call for us," he tells me. "Atti is ready to get you out in a second." Atti is my uncle in a way, or that's what I ended up calling him. Atti is also a witch, so he can appear anywhere he wants in a moment's notice. Witches are a pain in the ass to practice fighting against, considering they disappear and reappear in a new place every few seconds. Drives me nuts when Mich does that shit even now.

"Nothing is wrong. Everything is on plan. How is Winter?" I ask, changing the subject with the only subject I know he gets easily distracted by. Winter, his mate, my awesome stepmum. The queen of all the races and one Adie doesn't even seem to know about. How can she not know about the war? How can she not know about everything that happened when I was a kid? Winter fought for us all, defeating her father with the help of her four mates. I know none of us would be alive if it weren't for Winter and how brave she is. Everyone knows she is the direct descendant of a fate, a goddess—the goddess that made all the races. She was always destined to be our queen. My dad and her other mates saved us all too, they are the kings. There has been relative peace since the war, and only one enemy left to deal with. That's why this mission here is so important. It's to keep peace, something so many of my kind and family have died to find.

"Pregnant and eating chocolate, nothing new," he replies. "Though she is sleeping at the moment, or I'm sure she would want to say hello. Your aunt is here to help out with the gardens for the nature class at the school." Ah, that makes sense as to why she is at the castle. My aunt lives on the island, and I didn't expect her to be around, but if there are any issues with plants, my aunt can talk to them as one of her gifts. I used to think it was strange when I would find my aunt talking to flowers, trees and more as a kid, but you soon get used to it.

"Tell her hello from me and Josh. Tell dad I will call later in the week," I say. Uncle J doesn't say he will, but I know my uncle well enough to know he will tell them what I say.

"How is Josh coping?" Uncle J carefully asks. After what happened at the castle just before we left, I know he has good reason to worry. Uncle J has always been careful around Josh, though Winter never let Uncle J push him out. Neither did Atti who quickly became like a father to Josh.

"Good," I simply reply, even though it's not all truthful.

"Freddy, I know you're lying," Jaxson replies.

"He is keeping it under control. Chill out. I won't let him go all demon on my ass," I insist and rub my face, getting annoyed. We can't help what we are, and I won't let Josh destroy himself. I just wish Uncle Jaxson could see that. Only Winter and one of her mates, Atti, understand this. Everyone else is just frightened of him. "I have to go. Shit to do and all."

"Keep safe," Jaxson says, and I can tell from his tone he wants to warn me or say something stupid.

"Don't say it. Josh is a brother to me. End of story," I remind him. "What happened was an accident, and Nath can stop him if it happens again... which it won't."

"He is dangerous," Uncle J replies. "I only want you safe, and I don't think you can be safe with him at your side. Not until he learns to control that temper."

"A lot of people said that about Winter when they discovered what she is, yet you defended her," I remind him.

"It's not the same, and you know it," he tells me. Asshole.

"Later, Uncle J," I mutter and end the call. I slam the phone on the sofa, and it bounces off, hitting the floor and smashing into pieces. *Shit. I need another drink.*

FIVE

"Why can't I go to school again? Why do we have to stay here?" Sophie whines as she finishes her breakfast and just stares at me for an answer. *Someone got up on the wrong side of the bed this morning.*

"I told you, it isn't safe. We are leaving here next week and going somewhere that is safe. I am sure they will have a school for you there, with shifters like you," I tell her, before eating another spoonful of my cornflakes. Thank god we have one box of cereal and a carton of milk that I picked up from a gas station on the way. The next job is a big shop, and I have googled the local supermarket. Thankfully they have a decent sized Tesco in the village. After not sleeping well, I got up super early and spent the time unpacking the kitchen, bedroom and lounge. There is a box of spare things to go up in the attic, and I know I need to get brave and go up there at some point.

"Whatever. I don't want to go," she says. "Why do we always have to do what you want?!"

"Sophie, you know we have to be safe or we will be caught and likely dead before we can even blink. Trust me, this isn't what I want after just moving you here," I tell her. "The hunters are everywhere, and any chance to be safe, I have to take that. For us both. Imagine a life where you don't have to hide who you are and pretend to be human, when you are *not* one of them."

"I want to believe you, but I know you believed the shifter guy last night without a second thought. Even mum would have said that is dangerous," she states. I don't want to admit she is right, and I might have made a mistake trusting him. The instant bond we have is strange, and it's freaking me out, the more I think about it. The more I think about him. Since he left, I have this crazy urge to shift and run to find him. I'm sure that it is just my wolf hasn't shifted in a while, making her clearly crazy.

"He wasn't lying. I know it," I tell her instead of what I'm thinking.

"How?" she asks, tilting her head to the side a little as she stares at me.

"You can scent lies on people. It's a shifter thing," I say, shrugging my shoulders.

"I can't do that," she replies. "Neither could mum or dad. Or they would have caught me lying to them many times before." I go to say something, when I realise that I might have this ability from my birth parents, and I can't tell Sophie any of that.

"Some wolves get gifts, remember mum telling us that? Who knows, you might get a cool gift when you change at sixteen. Anyway, unless I'm looking for a lie, watching someone super closely, I can't always pick up a lie," I say. Not that I got anything or changed at all at sixteen. I've always been able to spot lies, move quickly, and my wolf is different than my parents' were. I don't even really look like a wolf when I shift. Mum always said it was normal, but now I think about it, I know it isn't.

"That's in eight months, and I doubt it will be anything cool," she mumbles.

"I miss us talking like this," I state, and I know I have said something wrong when she picks up her tablet, not looking at me, and slides off the table, walking to the door of the kitchen and pausing right before walking out.

"I'm going to stay in my room for the day. I have a lot to unpack," Sophie informs me, not looking back at me as she speaks. She opens the door and walks out, and I know there isn't anything I can say to stop her. I don't understand her reaction to me sometimes. She is grieving though, and no one, especially not a teenager, deals with grief well.

"Shit, I suck at this," I mutter to myself. I shake my head and quickly clean up the kitchen after breakfast. Looking at the nearly empty fridge, I know I can't put off shopping for much longer, so I grab my keys off the side.

"I'm going to the shops," I shout up the stairs as I slide my flat ballet shoes on by the door. I quickly pull my skinny jeans up my hips a little, as this pair always slips down which I like, being it makes me feel thin. I pull my light grey jumper into place and make sure my hair is smooth in the ponytail I put it up in earlier. I go to shout again when she finally replies.

"Bye," she shouts back down. *Well, at least it's a response.* I unlock the front door before walking out, and shutting it behind me. I glance at the house next door, the way it looks completely silent and still, and so much more modern than mine. Someone has taken the time to repaint it, replace the windows with double glazed ones and mow the lawn, which is a nice green colour. It looks much better than the yellow, overgrown grass on my front lawn. I suppose it doesn't matter when we are only staying here a week. There are three cars parked out front of the guys' house. Two of them are red, shiny, new and sporty. Not that I'd know the name of the car. They all look the same to me. The last one is more practical, bigger and painted black. The fourth guy must not have a car, or he is out or something. As I stare, I start to wonder if I can trust these complete strangers. Everything my parents ever taught me was to not trust people that aren't family. Then I remember the fact mum and dad lied to me my whole life, and never trusted me with the truth. Was Sophie right? Should I not trust these shifters? I quickly shuffle my feet to my own *falling apart* car, and after turning the key in the lock three times, it finally opens.

"Adie?" a male voice gently asks from a distance, and I turn a little, still holding the car door as a man walks over to me from the other house. This guy has dark blond hair that is lighter at the tips which I reckon he dyes. I don't look at his hair long though, because I'm distracted by his lack of shirt and the work out trousers which are dipping low on his hips.

A line of sweat makes his skin shimmer, and there is a pair of headphones in his hand attached to his phone. He must be a runner.

"Who are you?" I ask, keeping my hand tightly on the door for some kind of protection. When he gets closer and stops, I can smell that he is human, but I know he must be hiding it somehow like Rick did. I really need to find out how they hide who they are. I stare at the man, wondering why he seems so familiar to me. I find myself relaxing around him, even though he is a complete stranger.

"Nathaniel, but my friends call me Nath," he says, lifting a muscular arm and rubbing the back of his neck. I stare at him speechless for a little while, not picking up his scent no matter how much I try to make out what he is. *I suppose I could just ask.*

"Are you human?" I ask.

"Err, no. It's this," he points to his wrist, and I see the thick black leather bracelet that I didn't see before. "It has crystals in it that make me seem human."

"That must be useful in this kind of world," I muse, eyeing the bracelet.

"Very," he says, grinning as he lowers his arm, and we both smile at each other until he clears his throat. "Are you going out?"

"Yeah. I know Rick wanted me to come over in the morning, but we need food first," I explain.

"Rick wants you to have a protection bracelet on when you go to the village. Just in case. Can you come back to mine first, and then go out?" he asks. "It isn't safe. Don't make me have to follow you to the shops and kick anyone's ass who tries to attack you." I laugh, not sure if he is kidding or not because of the protective way he is staring at me.

"When you put it like that, coming to yours and getting a bracelet might be easier," I muse, and I enjoy how he seems happy.

"Damn, I was hoping we could spend more time together," he winks at me, making my cheeks go as bright red as my hair before nodding his head at the house. "Come on then, beautiful. Welcome to my home."

CHAPTER
SIX

"After you," Nath says, holding his front door open for me, and flashing me a seductive grin. Damn if it doesn't make my legs feel weak. I'm not used to hot guys. Not like Rick, Nath and even the scary Josh seem to be. Let's hope the last guy isn't this hot. I clear my throat before sliding past Nath into the cool feeling house. Unlike our house, someone has knocked the walls down on this floor, making it a huge open plan living/kitchen room, with a bar in the corner by the window. The staircase is in the middle, with a door on the side of it. There are brown leather sofas, a coffee table and a massive tv in the lounge area, and the kitchen has white counters, silver fridge and other silver appliances scattered around. I'm shocked at how tidy the house is when it has four guys living in it. I spot a basket of dirty clothes by the washing machine which has a load in and is turned on. Guys who know how to work a washing machine? That was practically unheard of in university. All the guys who were good looking had sticks up their asses and their parents to pay to make sure they didn't lift a finger.

"Can you wait down here while I get the bracelet?" Nath asks. I nod, and I stupidly decide to mutter under my breath.

"And a shirt so all women can breathe again."

"What was that? Keep my shirt off? No problem, beautiful," Nath comments, spinning around and winking at me before turning back and running up the stairs as I stare speechless. *I so didn't just say that.* I rub my arms as I look around the still room, spotting the half-opened packet of Oreo biscuits on the side. My tummy rumbles as I stare at them, knowing that the cornflakes did not fill the hole earlier. I suppose borrowing one Oreo couldn't hurt. I walk over and pull the wrapper back, sliding out one of the biscuits from heaven.

"Rick loves the shit out of those, you might not want to eat them all," Nath says, making me jump out my skin and turn as he gets to the bottom of the stairs. *How the hell did he move so silently?*

"Sorry, Oreos are hard to resist," I admit. "They are my favourite biscuits."

"Don't be sorry. No one else likes them, and Rick isn't here," Nath replies with a light chuckle, and I can't help but smile at the charming guy, "but we have another problem."

"What's up?" I ask.

"The bracelets aren't done yet, so that means you can't go into the village for food," Nath states. "Good news, we have lots of food here."

"I'm not borrowing your food. One trip into town isn't going to hurt," I say, finishing off the biscuit and walking to the door. I don't get close as Nath runs over and blocks my exit, his chest brushing against my arm and sending shivers through me.

"It could hurt if the wrong people see you there. Therefore, you can't go," he insists, folding his large arms across his still naked chest, and I gulp, forcing myself to look away from his muscular arms.

"Are you really going to try and stop me?" I ask, knowing my voice comes out more than a little flirty.

"It won't be trying, beautiful. You're a tiny girl

who might shift into a wolf, but I doubt you know how to fight your way past me," he retorts. I cross my own arms and glare up at him, knowing my wolf is thinking it's a good idea if I just shift and let her deal with the problem.

"I can't fight, but I sure can bite something if you don't move," I say, dropping my eyes to his crotch to make a point. When I look back up, Nath has the biggest grin on his face, and I know he isn't taking me seriously at all. We both look away from each other as the door opens behind Nath, and he steps to my side. I move away from him as his arm brushes against mine again, which seems to amuse him more. Rick frowns at us both as he comes in and shuts the door.

"What are you guys doing standing by the door?" he asks.

"Nothing," both Nath and I say at the same time, and I shake my head. "Adie needs to go food shopping, but the bracelet isn't ready yet. I suggested she borrow some of our food, but she still wants to go."

"You can't go," Rick agrees, looking at Nath as he talks and pretending like I'm not even here. "We should go and get the food she wants. It makes more sense."

"I didn't think of that. I will go and get a shirt," Nath states.

"I didn't say yes to you going for me!" I shout at Nath's back as he totally ignores me to run up the stairs.

"Look, we don't want the wrong people seeing you and telling the hunters. I'm sure you want the same thing, so let us go. It's only one day and then you have the bracelets, and you can go wherever you like," he says to me, sounding reasonable which is so hard to argue with.

"Alright, fine. Is there anything I can do around the house to repay you for going?" I ask.

"Well first off, you can write a list and text me it. Hand me your phone a sec," he asks, and I slide it out my jean pocket and hand it to him.

"Password," he asks, with a little smile.

"I'm not telling you that. Just turn it to look at me. It has that face scanner thingy," I say, and Rick turns the phone, which unlocks after I slide it open.

"It was worth a shot. I want to get to know you, and people's passwords usually say a lot about them," Rick says, typing numbers into my phone.

"How so?" I ask.

"Say the person's password is their pet's name. You know the thing they love the most in a second.

Say it was their children's, you know their favourite or only child means the most...but what if it was a brand name? Like the name of their car make. You then learn that person cares more about his car than anything else," he tells me, never looking up once.

"What is your password?" I ask.

"It's a secret, Red. One I might tell you one day," he winks at me before handing me the phone back, locking his blue eyes on mine.

"I'm going to get a bottle of water while you make a list. Then maybe you could help me with something," he tells me and walks off after I nod. I quickly type a list and search for Rick's number. I laugh when I see he has put his number as "Rick, the one I fell for." I send him the list just as he walks back to me.

"I like it when you smile, Red," he remarks and nods his head towards the stairs. "Come up."

"What exactly do you want me to do?" I ask, following him up the stairs.

"I need you to watch someone. We don't ever leave her alone in the house...not after last time," he pauses, looking like he was going to tell me the situation and then changes his mind, and waits for me at the top of the stairs. "Anyways, Nath and I will go to the store. Mich and Josh are out, so we need a babysitter of sorts."

"Babysitting I can do," I say. I wonder how old the child is and if any of the guys are the parents. "Which one of you is her dad?"

"Oh, none of us, but she is kinda like our child," Rick laughs, walking down the hallway with cream painted walls and dark wooden floors. "We are all recently single if you were wondering."

"All of you at the same time are recently single?" I ask.

"We like to share sometimes," Rick says, winking at me as I stare wide-eyed at what he is suggesting. Rick doesn't seem to notice my shock as he opens the third door in the corridor, and walks in. I follow him into the room that is clearly his bedroom. There are clothes on the wooden floor, which he quickly picks up and throws in a washing basket.

"Sorry, I don't usually have company," he admits, picking up more clothes.

"I'm usually messier, so don't worry," I say and freeze when I hear a light snoring noise.

"What is that?" I ask, staring at the little pink creature sleeping in Rick's dark wooden bed. The creature is so small that her whole body is on the white pillow, and she has the sheet tightly wrapped around her. I move closer, staring at her sparkly pink hair that matches her light pink skin. She has little pink wings that look like the wings from a butterfly. *Oh my god, she reminds me of Tinkerbell, only not blonde. Is she a fairy?*

"Tay, a pixie. Please, for your own sake, don't let her get hold of any alcohol while we are gone," Rick warns me, picking up his wallet off a box at the end of the bed.

"Why?" I slowly ask, staring at the innocent creature. *She is so cute.*

"You don't want to know, Red, you really don't," he chuckles, walking out of the room. *Well, that isn't worrying at all.* I run and catch up with him just before he goes downstairs.

"Don't you need my bank card for the food?" I ask, going to find it in my bag.

"Nope. Consider it a moving-in gift," Rick says and runs down the stairs before I can even say no. Nath comes out his room, a pair of keys in his hand, a white shirt covering his chest up, and grins at me.

"Good luck with Tay," he laughs. I look back at the small creature. *How could anything that innocent looking be that hard to watch?*

CHAPTER
SEVEN

"Stop throwing things at me! You crazy little pixie!" I shout at her, ducking with a squeak as she throws a cup at my head and it smashes into pieces on the wall just above me. I run out of the kitchen and towards the sofa, hiding behind it. I glance around the sofa, seeing the pixie is looking for something else to throw at me. *That cute little thing is evil.* Since the—not so innocent after all—pixie woke up, all she has done is throw things at me. At first, I thought the pillow throwing was cute, but when she decided to pick up much heavier things, it wasn't so cute after all.

"Go!" the pixie demands, her voice sweet and sugary, and far too bloody close for my liking. I peek over the sofa, and she is flying, holding a sharp knife not far away.

"Right, this has gone way too far! Damn Rick for not explaining you are psycho, pixie! I'm not leaving, and if you don't put that knife down right now, I am going to shift and let my wolf eat you," I say, standing up off the floor and holding my hands on hips. Tay looks at the knife and back to me, seriously debating my words.

"Rick?" she asks, the affection for him clear in her tone.

"Rick asked me to watch you while he runs to the shops," I reply, and she drops the knife and grins, looking me up and down.

"Be gone," she retorts, and I can tell she is jealous. *Am I really arguing with a tiny, pink, glittery pixie?*

"I'm not going anywhere," I dryly reply, and she tilts her tiny little head to the side before raising her hands and transforming into an owl. The owl is white, with pink feathers laced into the fur. Tay, the owl, flies off up the stairs, and I collapse onto the sofa, resting my head back. I don't know if I should be proud that I won a fight with a pixie the size of my hand, but I am. *I so am.* I pull my phone out and text Sophie to check she is okay, and I only get a simple thumbs up emoji as a reply. *Nice.* I glance around at the now trashed room and know I should clean it up. Even if it was their fault for not telling me about the crazy pixie who can throw like a quarterback. I pick the knife up and slide it back into the drawer that is left open in the kitchen. I find a broom resting by the back door and quickly start sweeping up all the broken cups, glasses and plates. Just as I finish getting it all into a pile, the doorbell rings. As I wonder if I should answer it, they ring again, and I sigh, knowing I should. I rest the broom against the wall. I run to the door and open it. A man resting on a walking stick stands completely still as he smiles at me. The man is older, about fifty I believe, with short grey hair and brown eyes. He has a brown suit on, and I glance at the walking stick that he heavily leans on, seeing a yellow crystal on top, cut out in the shape of a dragon. I scent him as completely human.

"Hi! Can I help you?" I ask, holding onto the door.

"I'm looking for Rick, Mich, Nath or Josh. Are any of them in?" he replies, looking behind me.

"No, sorry. They just popped out," I explain.

"Who are you? I say, we don't see many new

people around here and none as lovely as you are," he asks, and I laugh.

"I'm new to town. My name is Adelaide," I say and hold out a hand. He grabs my hand rather roughly to shake, just as a car pulls into the drive. Josh smoothly gets out the black sports car I haven't seen before, his dark eyes locking on me for a moment before looking over at the man.

"Josh. Perfect timing," the man says as Josh runs up the path and stands next to the man.

"Mr. Graves. I didn't expect to see you at my home," Josh says, and Mr. Graves slowly lets my hand fall and pulls his eyes off me.

"I wanted to check in on you after the mission this morning. I know it wasn't easy capturing that family. The life of hunters can be a hard job. I should know, half my body is burnt due to a shifter," Mr. Graves says calmly, but everything in me starts to panic as I try to process what he just said. I glance back down at the yellow dragon, and remember the symbol advertised everywhere since Paris fell. The sign of the Hunter's Organisation. They are hunters. Why would these supernaturals be hunters unless they like to hunt their own kind.

"Capturing?" I whisper.

"Yes, a family of witches. Josh and the others are our finest hunters," Mr. Graves muses, watching me closely. "Good hunters are always hard to find these days."

"I imagine. They need to be good at lying and keeping secrets, I suppose," I say, keeping my eyes locked with Josh's so he knows that sentence was meant for him and his friends. He looks more and more pissed off by the second.

"Ah, I feel we could get along. How do you two know each other?" Mr. Graves asks.

"Adelaide is our...cousin...distant cousin who needed a place to stay," Josh smoothly answers, only pausing a little bit to make up a lie. He must be used to lying to make something up on the spot and seem so convincing as he says it.

"Now, I do like people who look after their own. Do you have a job yet, Adelaide? I imagine it is hard to find work in this small village, and it is such a drive to the main town," Mr. Graves asks me, and I can only shake my head for an answer, pulling my eyes from Josh to Mr. Graves.

"N-no," I clear my throat. "No, I haven't had a chance to look for a job yet, but it is my plan to find one soon."

"My receptionist is having a baby, and I need to find a local person for a replacement. What do you say to working with me?" he suggests. "I certainly pay well."

"You're offering me a job?" I ask, a little thrown back in shock.

"Well, I want to help the cousin of my best hunters. It might make them stay in my division a little longer and ignore those head-hunters who will likely pay them more," he says, and both Josh and he laugh. Though Josh's couldn't sound more fake if he tried.

"Can I have some time to think on it?" I ask, feeling more than a little nervous now. I'm a shifter. I can't work for the hunters like my crazy ass neighbours.

"Of course! Why doesn't one of your cousins bring you in for a tour tomorrow, and you can decide if you like it," he suggests.

"Sounds perfect," I say slowly, and he grins.

"Yes, it does. I will see you at base, Josh," Mr. Graves says. "Lovely to meet you, Adelaide. Such an unusual name you have there." I smile tightly and watch as he turns, waking down the path. He gets into the white Jeep with dark windows I can't see through before driving off.

"You have no fucking idea what you just did," Josh growls, and I cross my arms, growling low as his eyes glow.

"Don't threaten me," I snap.

"Or what?"

CHAPTER

EIGHT

"What the fuck is going on?" Rick exclaims, and my wolf turns her head, looking over at Rick and Nath standing in the doorway with bags of shopping in their hands. My wolf looks back down at Josh, who is underneath her and who she has been fighting with for the last ten minutes. Well, I wouldn't say fighting, not when Josh has been pushing me away like I'm a puppy. Josh laughs, pushing me off him in one smooth movement.

"Adie lost her temper, shifted and tried to bite me," Josh explains, fixing his crumpled shirt.

"And you didn't knock her out?" Rick asks, sounding a little shocked. I growl, shaking my head as Josh smirks at me. I can't be knocked out that easy.

"I didn't want to hurt her, so I let her play for a bit," Josh states, and my wolf sits back, feeling more than a little annoyed.

"Adie, your wolf..." Nath murmurs, and I remember how strange my wolf must look to them. My back is black with blue lines swirled into the fur. I have a strange circle of blue swirls on my forehead and my ears are pointy. Like seriously tall. It makes it so I can hear miles away while I'm in this form, but I don't have a clue what the blue swirls are for or from. After reading that letter from mum, I'm guessing it's a Fray thing. I glance at my foot, seeing that the red bracelet has stayed on and is attached around my leg, just before my right paw.

"Is weird right?" Josh remarks, smoothing down his messy hair. My wolf steps closer, baring her teeth with a long growl.

"Not weird. Just different," Rick suggests, interrupting my wolf's thoughts as she watches Rick instead. He puts the shopping bag on the floor, walking slowly over to me. "I've never seen a wolf that looks like you."

"The ears make her look like a cat," Josh remarks, and I growl once again.

"Josh, why don't you go to Adie's with Nath, and get some clothes for her," Rick suggests, but it comes out as more of a growl. Nath opens the door, and Josh looks between us with an annoyed frown.

"Whatever," Josh replies emotionlessly and walks out the door after Nath, shutting it behind him.

"Shift back so we can talk?" Rick asks and picks a blanket up off the back of one of the sofas and places it in front of me. "I will turn around and wait." I pull my wolf back and shake off the light pain from the change before grabbing the blanket and wrapping it around me. When it's secure, I reach and touch Rick's shoulder, so he can turn. He goes to say something, but I put my hand up.

"Oh, I can start off," I growl out. "One, the wild ass pixie spent half an hour throwing things at me, and you could have warned me about that ball of crazy! Two, you are working for the hunters? Are you insane or do you actually hunt your own kind?"

"If I hunted my own kind, do you really think I would be protecting you?" he asks, not seeming bothered about my outbreak. "And I am sorry about Tay. We will go back to that one later after I've had a word with her."

"What are you doing then?" I ask, needing to

understand why they are working with hunters. Hunters are nasty people. The videos on YouTube of what they have done to my kind, it is horrible. Hunters take pleasure in hunting us and have the backing of a world full of scared humans.

"How do you know we are working for the hunters?" he asks.

"Mr. Graves came here and told me. He offered me a job...and I have to go into the base to be shown around tomorrow," I tell him, and his eyes widen in shock.

"Fucking hell," he mutters, rubbing the back of his head. The front door opens again, and this time a guy I haven't seen walks in, stopping when he sees me in just a blanket. He raises his dark eyebrows at Rick.

"Adie, this is Mich," Rick introduces us, pronouncing Mich like Mitch. Mich has short brown-nearly-black hair and dark eyes. He has a business looking suit on, that goes well with his serious expression. He has a smoothly shaven face, and he is just as good looking as his friends. I can't scent him as anything other than human, and even then he smells good.

"The wolf?" Mich asks, his voice is husky and deep, and not impressed. "Sleeping with her already? I thought you were sending her away from here, not keeping her. Now is not the time to be fucking around, Rick."

"I've just met you all, and you think I would sleep with any of you that quickly?" I ask.

"You are in just a blanket," he responds.

"I shifted...and ripped my clothes over there," I point at the pile of clothes, and he doesn't even bother looking.

"You are going to be trouble for us all," Mich remarks, looking at me like I stole his steak off his dinner plate before literally disappearing into thin air.

"What the hell?" I ask, staring at where Mich literally just was.

"Witches. Well, Mich is a half witch, half shifter," Rick explains. "Do you not know about other kinds?"

"I know witches, angels, shifters and vampires exist. Just not their powers," I explain.

"Well, we are all half breeds here. I'm half shifter and half vampire," he tells me. "The others you will have to guess." He winks.

"Do you drink blood?" I ask, curious if he needs it.

"Yes. Only once or twice a month," he explains.

"I didn't know half breeds were a thing, but it makes sense," I say, and Nath walks through the door with a pile of clothes and is rubbing the side of his head where a cut is healing.

"Your sister wasn't happy about us coming over, and she threw a shoe at my head," Nath explains, handing me the clothes as I try not to laugh.

"The bathroom is down there, under the stairs," Rick points and whacks Nath on the arm. I walk away but still hear Rick speaking quietly to Nath. "You got beat up by a tiny girl, seriously, man? Way to look cool."

I chuckle as I pull the bathroom door open and step inside, shutting the door and taking a deep breath as I make a mental plan. Get changed. Find out why they are working for hunters. If they are the bad guys...*run.*

CHAPTER
NINE

"Thanks," I say as Nath hands me a cup of tea, and Rick offers me a chocolate bar from the bags of shopping. I've already eaten Rick's Oreos, which Nath seemed really surprised that Rick would share them with me. These last few days have just been insane, and I literally have no idea how to process it. Mum and dad aren't my real parents. There is somewhere safe for shifters to live. Pixies are real, cute and crazy. I wasn't born on Earth, and my neighbours are hunters. Safe to say, I need more than a cup of tea and chocolate to get my head around all of this. Being at university and studying history seems like years ago now.

"Chocolate always makes things better," Rick

explains. I'm surprised that he knows that. Guys don't usually seem to care.

"Do you want some?" I ask as Nath sits next to Rick on the sofa.

"My stepmum, Winter, loves chocolate too. We learnt very quickly that no one comes between a woman and her chocolate... not unless you want an angry, crazy person chasing you," Rick says, and Nath nods his agreement, a look of fear crossing over their faces. "So, it's all yours." *This Winter sounds awesome, and I can't wait to meet her.* I pop some more chocolate in my mouth, trying not to laugh.

"Well, thanks...but I still need some real answers about the hunters," I remark, putting the chocolate bar on the coffee table and wrapping my hands around the warm cup as I watch them for answers.

"Ten years ago, Paris fell," Nath starts off and pauses as I nod my head.

"I know. *Everyone* knows that," I reply.

"Let me tell the story then, smartass," Nath retorts, and I chuckle. "There was a big war between the supernaturals and demons. Demons were the creatures that destroyed Paris, not the supernaturals like the world has everyone believing."

"I didn't know demons existed," I reply. I can't imagine they are nice things to be around.

"Demons are from hell, and they can possess other people's bodies, amongst other things. Queen Winter and her four mates won the war, sent the demons back to hell, and closed the only portal. After that, Earth knew of supernaturals and wanted revenge for the millions of people that died," he tells me. When Paris was destroyed, mum and dad had moved us to Spain, and we hid well. Regardless, life changed for everyone overnight.

"They wanted a way to make sure it never happened again, and the Hunter's Organisation stepped up," Rick carries on the story, "being the heroes everyone wanted by destroying the creatures and people they feared."

"The Hunter's Organisation was once a private business that was small, and they hunted supernaturals in secret. After Paris, they got the backing of the governments all over the world and started to grow in mass numbers," Nath fills in what I always suspected happened with them. About a year after Paris, adverts looking for people to hire for hunters appeared all over TV and the internet. There were also warnings, ways to look for people that were different and where to find them.

"They attacked any supernatural. They took them, experimented on them and killed them. So, Winter and the kings attacked them back, destroying as many places as they could find and taking back our people in the beginning," Rick tells me.

"But that didn't stop the hunters," I finish his story.

"No, it had the bad effect of making the hunters more popular. They got more money, they grew faster, and Winter was forced to back off because it was putting everyone at risk," he explains.

"So how are you guys involved now?" I ask.

"Winter wasn't stupid, she never has been, and she never gives up on her own people. She knew that the best way to take down any organisation is having spies and learning how to take them down from the inside rather than blindly attacking," Rick answers.

"That's what you are?" I ask.

"Kind of, but not exactly. Winter has spies in every organisation in the world now, except for the one in this village. The one here is the main base, with the most secrets and extreme tests to get hired. We have spent months getting in and getting close to Mr. Graves who leads everything. Yet, he doesn't trust us, and we can't figure out how to get him to," Nath explains, seeming frustrated.

"What is the plan then?" I ask.

"There are ten floors to the base, and we need to evacuate every floor at the same time, and then blow the place up. Every spy is ready to do the same across the entire world, and put the hunters out of business for good," Rick tells me. "This has been planned for a long time...we can't mess it up. There are thousands of lives on the line."

"I don't understand why you can't just go ahead with the plan now," I ask. They are already hunters, and they are already inside the base every day, it seems, for work. What are they waiting for? Surely every day is dangerous in case they get caught.

"Only Mr. Graves's closest hunters go to the last two floors. We can't get the codes for them, not until he trusts us more than he does right now," Nath replies to me. "If we make the plan, we need the codes, or we can't rescue anyone, and the mission would be for nothing."

"Once you get the codes?" I ask.

"We set a date and then boom, we finish our mission and go home to our people," Rick says with a big smile that slowly drifts into a more serious frown as he looks at me. "The problem now is you."

"Me?" I whisper.

"Mr. Graves invited you to work with him, and if we send you to the castle, and you just disappear... he isn't going to take that well," Rick practically growls, sounding extremely over protective and worried about me at the same time. Nath briefly glances at his friend with a confused look before blanking his expression. I don't know what is up with Rick, but I don't need some protective alpha right now. I'm sure he is just worried about the chance of me messing up their mission.

"I can't stay near a hunter base with my sister," I remark. "We have to leave."

"I'm not suggesting Sophie stays," Rick lightly tells me, and I pick up on his unspoken statement.

"But you're suggesting I do?" I ask.

"Yes," Rick answers. "Just for a month, and then you can say you miss home and want to go back. Make some excuse up, and you can then leave."

"That can't be safe."

"I will never let anything happen to you, none of us will. Anytime you are there, we will be near you and keeping watch," Rick firmly tells me, and I don't doubt him, but the idea of going into a hunter base is terrifying.

"I don't have a choice, do I?" I whisper.

G. BAILEY

"You do. If you want to go, you can go to the castle, and we will leave the mission. But it will cost a lot of innocent people's lives. There are over fifty supernaturals kept in that base that we have seen go in, and god knows how many were in there before we got the job," Rick replies. One look into his blue eyes, and I know he means it. If I don't want to do this, I can just walk away, but that would be a coward's actions. *I'm no coward.* If it was the other way around, and I was locked in a hunter base, I would want someone to save me. These guys are doing the right thing, and I can't walk away, forcing them to give it up. I'd hate myself, and they would no doubt hate me too.

"Then I will stay to help, but you have to promise me that you will protect me if something goes wrong," I ask.

"I will always protect you. I promise," Rick says.

"Same," Nath answers, staring at me intently as I sip on my cup of tea, wishing the warm drink would somehow make me feel better about all of this.

"Then I best go home and tell Sophie the news," I eventually say.

"Sophie will love the castle. My stepmum's best friend has a daughter who's nearly the same age as Sophie, and a total troublemaker. She will make friends, and it's only going to be one month until you are back with her," Rick tries to comfort me, but it's hard not to worry.

"Sophie has lost her parents, all her friends and her old home. Now I'm about to tell her she won't see her sister for a while, and she has to leave…it isn't going to go well, no matter what I say to her," I reply.

"Let's hope she doesn't throw anything at you," Nath says, rubbing his head even though the bump has healed. I smile internally.

"I'll be sure to hide the shoes," I can't resist but say, and Nath glares at me. "After all, they are scary in the hands of a little girl." Rick laughs, while Nath doesn't look at all impressed. I finish drinking my tea before leaving the cup on the coffee table and standing up.

"From now on, one of us will be at your house at all times. For safety reasons," Rick informs me, and Nath nods in agreement. "No more risks."

"I will go over to stay tonight. Let me just grab the bracelets and the crystals to work on, and some pajamas," Nath says and jogs to the stairs before I can even tell him no.

"I didn't even agree to letting him stay," I protest. "Or any of you to stay for that matter." Rick walks around the coffee table to me and places his hand on my shoulder. The little contact sends shivers all over me, and I can't help but focus on how nice his hand feels.

"Let us keep you safe. If anything happened to you, none of us would ever be able to forgive ourselves," he urges, his voice gentle, and I stare into his blue eyes that are brighter than I thought they were.

"Okay," I find myself saying, and he slowly slides his hand down my arm, sending goose bumps and making me shiver all over again. If he knows the effect he is having on me, he doesn't show it. I'm sure a guy that looks like him and is a prince, is used to this effect on women.

"Thank you, Adie," he grins, removing his hand and walking around me to the piles of shopping. "I will carry your shopping back for you. Let's go home, Nath can catch up." *Why do I like him calling my house home?*

"Sophie, come on. You know I'm right," I plead with her, even though my reasoning isn't getting through to her, despite how many times I've told her my explanation of why she has to leave and I have to stay.

"NO! I hate you! You're leaving me alone and sending me away! Why would you do this to me?!" she shouts through the locked bedroom door. I slide down the door, wrapping my arms around my legs and resting my head back against it.

"You don't hate me, or you wouldn't be so upset about this," I retort, hearing her cry and wishing she would open the door. I could break it down with one kick, but it's not the point. She needs to let me in.

And I also don't want to fix a broken door as I have no clue how to do that.

"I'm scared," she whispers through sobs, my shifter hearing just barely picking up on it.

"I know you are, and I am too. I'm scared that if I'm selfish and keep you here with me, you will be killed. I'm scared that you will really hate me for making you leave, even though it is the right thing to do," I explain my feelings to her, hoping it will make her understand. "I'm most scared that I'm letting mum and dad down in some way by making the right choice and letting you go."

"I don't hate you. I'm sorry I said that," I hear her mumble, and it's surprising how relieved I am to hear her say it.

"I know you don't hate me, sis. It's only one month, and I will be back. Just one month. Mum and dad raised you to be strong, just like they raised me to be. I know you can do this," I reply and hear her footsteps across the room as I pull myself to my feet. Sophie opens the door and flings herself into my arms, holding me tight as she cries.

"Mum and dad went out, leaving me with a babysitter for a few days, and they promised they would come back...they didn't come back. I don't want you to not come back," she whispers, but my sensitive hearing picks it up, and she knows I can hear her.

"I am coming back, Sophie. I will be back, and you can show me all around the castle, and no doubt introduce me to the friends you will make there," I tell her, and she lets me go, nodding rapidly before wiping her eyes.

"Did you bring food back? I'm hungry," she remarks, clearly wanting to change the subject, and I awkwardly laugh.

"Yes, I just put it all away, and Nath is making sandwiches for us," I say.

"Who is Nath, and why is he here?" she asks, crossing her arms.

"Nath is one of the neighbours, and different like us. He will be staying tonight for protection. One of them will be staying here every night," I tell her, and she bites her nails, clearly thinking it over. "Why don't you go down and ask if he needs help? I'm going to put some of the spare things in the attic before I come down."

"Okay. As long as he isn't messy, can cook, and puts the toilet seat down, then he can stay," she says.

"Why don't you tell him your demands as he makes you food? I'm sure he can comply with them,"

I say, biting my lip, trying not to laugh at the thought of Sophie telling Nath what to do after she threw a shoe at him. She nods, clearly thinking that it's a good idea, and walks past me to go down the stairs.

I go to my room and pick up the box of spare things I want to put in the attic, knowing I've put off going up there long enough. The whole reason mum and dad left us this house was for whatever they hid up there. I walk back to the corridor and put the box on the floor before reaching up for the attic door. I pull the door down, revealing the ladder stairs, which easily slide down to the ground. After climbing up the steps, I look around the dark attic for any sign of a light. I reach into my pocket and pull my phone out, turning the flash on and using it to find a switch for the light. The switch isn't far away; I reach over turning it on, and it lights up the massive room. I climb up the final steps and climb onto the floor which has carpet done. I stare around at the room which is full of old-looking boxes and one massive desk covered in books. I walk to the desk, first sitting down on the old chair which squeaks from the movement. Each of the books looks ancient, and I'm half scared to open them in case they fall apart.

One of the books is open right in front of me, and I blow on it to get rid of the dust. I use my hand to smooth away some more of the dust and see the drawing of a woman stood in the middle of a field. The woman has long purple hair and matching purple wings. She has purple flowers tattooed all up her arms, matching the purple trees in the background. Just underneath the woman is the subscript 'the Queen of the Spring court'. *What the hell is a Spring court?* I wipe the other side of the book down with the back of my cardigan sleeve and stare down at the words—well, symbols—which for a second don't seem to make any sense, when suddenly I can actually read them.

The Frayan world was said to be the first of all the worlds created. At first, they say only gods, goddesses, and fates lived alone on the planet which was more beautiful than life itself. Eventually, they all got tired of living lives of luxury all alone. They began making animals for companions, and small creatures only they could speak to, but this didn't keep them amused for long. The gods decided to make different worlds and leave. Four gods and goddesses remained with four fates as their mates. They made the courts of Frayan as they spilt the land in

four sections to live out their lives. Each of them had a child born in a different season. One child was born in winter, one child was born in spring, one child was born in autumn, and finally, one child was born in summer. Each child became the heir to the court they were born in. This is the start of the Frayan courts. The gods made the Fray race so that their children could have further children and continue the courts, but only the royal blood line carried the blessing of the wings.
This is how the Frayan race began and how it has always been for thousands of years, long after the fates and gods disappeared from all worlds.

I GO to turn the page when I hear someone shout my name and recognise it as Sophie. Frayan sounds like a beautiful place and like a fairy tale. Who knows if any of this is right or real? I stand up and look around all the boxes knowing that they must hold the history of the race I have just read about. The race which my mum says I came from. This must be the way she wanted me to learn my history, learn who my parents are maybe. Though looking at the dozens of boxes, it is going to take me a long time to go through them all and have any understanding of the Frayan world. I shake my head and climb back down the ladder, picking up the box and taking it up to the attic before turning the light off and closing it. Covered in dust, I pull my cardigan off and hang it over the banister. Then I shake my hair to get the dust out before running downstairs. I follow the sounds of talking to the kitchen, when the door is held open by a doorstop. Sophie and Nath are eating sandwiches on plates and quietly talking as I walk in.

"For you," Nath says, holding out a plate he slides off the side. The sandwich is thick with cheese, ham, and salad. It looks really nice.

"Thanks. What were you guys talking about?" I ask, seeing Sophie's smile.

"Nath was telling me about the castle and about the war. He was explaining what his life was like there as a kid," Sophie fills me in.

"What about it?" I ask, before taking a bite of my sandwich, interested to know what a place is like with just supernaturals living in it.

"I moved into the castle in the middle of war, and mother was rewarded a place on the council, which I inherited a few years back. The council runs the everyday issues that come up, but anything serious, the queen and kings will take over. They always have the final say in any situation, but after the war, there weren't many serious things that came up. Most of us were thankful to be alive and respected the royals for fighting for us, therefore it got pretty boring for us as kids," Nath says, grinning at me before taking a bite of his own sandwich.

"Bored supernatural kids...that couldn't have been easy to handle," I say, looking at Sophie. One is bad enough. I couldn't imagine a whole castle full of them.

"Yeah, we got into a lot of trouble and always had our families chasing us. Practical jokes mixed with magic," Nath winks at me, "well it was fun until we got caught." I laugh with Sophie and Nath, enjoying seeing Sophie so interested in anything other than her iPad.

"You said there is a school?" I ask.

"The Royal School for All Supernaturals. I know, it's a mouth full of a name. The castle has been transformed into a school as it is the safest place, and the surrounding lands have cabins for housing. The school has only recently opened as we had to relocate a lot of our people to the island," Nath explains.

"Island?" I ask.

"Ever heard of Atlantis? It's not just a story," Nath says, grinning at Sophie's shocked face.

"Atlantis is real?" she asks in awe.

"Yep. Once you are at the castle, you can go and visit it. There are portals in the castle that open on weekends for kids to go back home and see their families. Or just to go shopping on the island, go to the beaches, see the jewel trees and anything they want to do," Nath says. "The island is something I can't wait to show Adie. All women love it."

"How old are the kids that go to the school?" I ask, ignoring how he just suggested something like a date and his flirty tone.

"Fifteen to twenty-one. That's the time that most supernaturals need help with their new powers, and need to learn a bit of independence," Nath explains. "It will also help promote interacting between races that used to be completely apart."

"How old are you?" Sophie asks.

"I'm the baby of the group, only twenty-three," he says. "The rest of the guys are all twenty-five or twenty-six," he says, and puts his empty plate on the side.

"I think I'm going to like this castle. Or at least try to," Sophie says with a sigh. "Though I hate strict schools, but at least I won't have to hide my wolf and be scared of what seems normal to me."

"I know what it is like to be alone and not around people that understand you. The castle will be full of people your age, looking for their own pack, their own family to fight for, to love and to protect. It's our nature to search for that," Nath gently replies, though his eyes stay on me as he says it. I feel like the message was for me, and I don't really know how to respond to it. It makes me feel vulnerable and alone, which I don't like.

"He basically means you might make some friends," I say, joking a bit with Sophie. "Friends other than your iPad, that is."

"Maybe," Sophie says, trying to hide her little smile from me. "I'm going to eat in the lounge." Nath doesn't say anything as I finish my sandwich and Sophie leaves. I put the empty plate on top of his on the side.

"Thanks for that. It was really nice. I didn't realise how hungry I was," I tell him.

"Don't worry about it. I grew up around shifters, I know we need more food than most," he says as I look at the empty doorway for a second and look back at Nath who is watching me closely. "Sophie is a good kid and she will fit in well at the castle."

"Yeah, I hope so. My parents were amazing people, so I'm not surprised she grew up to be lovely and strong," I tell him.

"Much like her sister," Nath muses, looking like he wants to say something before he blurts out, "Can I ask you something though?"

"What?" I ask, going to the sink where I start washing the plates off.

"I know you are half Fray...like me. I can sense my own kind, though you are a little different, but I bet that's your wolf side interfering somehow," he muses. "Do you know what being Fray is? What you are? Does Sophie know?"

"That's more than one question there, Nath," I awkwardly chuckle, looking over my shoulder at him and seeing no judgement. I'm a little shocked he is half Fray...but considering today is full of shocks, I'm getting used to it. I hoped one of them would know something about Fray, and asking them was part of my plan. "No, Sophie doesn't know, and I didn't know until recently. I don't even know what I am. What being Fray is."

"Fray are like fairies and they have weather magic and energy magic. That's literally all I know. My mum won't speak about my dad much. There are Fray who came here in the war, but they don't speak about their past or Frayan," he says. "They say it's too painful as they miss their home. Earth apparently does not compare to Frayan."

"Then maybe there is something you can help me with. Maybe you can find answers too, if you want to," I muse, leaving the plates and nodding my head towards the door, before walking out with Nath following me. *Two pairs of eyes are always better than one.*

CHAPTER ELEVEN

"Are you going to murder me in the attic?" Nath says as he climbs up the ladder and has to duck his head a little from the slanted ceiling because he is built like a tree. "I saw a movie where that happened once."

"You just made me food, so you're safe," I joke, and he grins, before looking around the room with more interest now we are up here.

"So why are we here?" he slowly asks, and I nod my head towards the desk.

"Look at this," I say, pointing at the book. Nath slides into the seat, and starts reading the passage, and I silently wait for him to finish.

"I didn't know any of this. Mum once said my dad was a guard of the Winter court," Nath whispers quietly. "It never made any sense, and she didn't know what a Winter court was, so we never had answers."

"My mum left me a note, telling me I was born on Frayan and that she wasn't my mother. That my dad wasn't my father. The note said I would find answers here...but there is a lot to go through," I say, seeing the slightly sympathetic look Nath flashes me before I look at the boxes. "I don't even know where to start or what to believe."

"I'm sorry they didn't tell you who you are before they passed away," Nath lightly whispers, but in the silent room, it sounds louder than it should. "I bet it would have been easier to hear them tell you the truth."

"Mum said she was blood bound to never tell me the truth," I inform him because I don't want anyone thinking badly of her, and a look of understanding flashes in his eyes. I don't understand what blood bound means, but I'm sure Nath does.

"I think we should tell my friends—" he starts off.

"No. I'm trusting you because you are like me and want answers...they aren't like us. I don't want to risk Sophie hearing any of this, and I'm not ready to talk to anyone else," I quickly tell him. "I don't even know why I shared this with you, but here we are."

"You don't have to say anymore, Adie. This can be our secret," Nath says, being serious for a second, and I really appreciate it.

"Thank you," I lightly whisper back. "Don't you think it is strange how we trust each other so quickly?"

"Not really. When I first met Rick, Mich, and Josh, we trusted each other from the get go. It is the same with you, maybe some part of us deep down knows that we can trust each other," he muses. "Either way, I'm interested to see what's inside all these boxes."

"Me too. My mum wouldn't have left all these boxes for me if there wasn't something interesting in them," I reply, and tuck a little bit of my hair behind my ear, catching a little strand of my hair in the bracelet on my wrist.

"Ouch," I say, slowly pulling my hair out of the bracelet, somehow getting it more stuck. I look up as Nath takes over, pulling the strand out effortlessly and letting it fall as he looks down at me. There is a moment where we both just stare, speechless, and in a trance of sorts. The small contact of his hand holding my arm feels like lightning is buzzing through my skin, and I really never noticed how seductive everything is about Nath. The way his tanned skin is the perfect shade, how his hair looks silky soft and the way his green eyes are so deep that anyone could get lost while they stared into them. It's not just his attractive body that makes him seductive, it's everything.

"Where is this from?" Nath asks gently, rubbing a thumb over the bracelet and snapping me out of it. I look down at where his hand rests on the bracelet and at the three red crystals that almost shimmer under his touch.

"My mum said it belonged to my biological father," I say, "and I suspect it's from Frayan. I have no idea what it is, but I think I need to keep it on."

"One of my powers is to control energy. It's how I make the jewelry that makes us seem human. I also have an extremely high connection to crystals and the energy they produce. If you would let me, I could find out what kind of energy this crystal has," he says. "Some crystals can talk and even hold messages."

"What energies do crystals usually have?" I ask. "And how do they keep messages?"

"Protection. Healing. They can even hold element powers for attacking or defending yourself," he explains to me. "I only need you to hold your arm out, and I can check if there is anything interesting in these crystals."

"What's the worst that could happen?" I reply.

"You shouldn't say that. Every time anyone says that, something goes wrong," he jokes, making me laugh as I hold my arm out and he steps back a little. I watch, silent, as he hovers his joined hands over the crystals. His hands start to glow, a light blue haze appearing around them, and it spreads down to cover the bracelet. The red crystals start to glow brightly, and I scream as shooting pain spreads up my arm, making me drop to the floor as the waves of pain continue to spread from it.

"Adie!" Nath drops to my side, pulling me onto his lap, and the pain slowly fades as I focus on the sound of his heartbeat near my ear which is pressed against his warm chest. I take deep breaths as I try not to cry from the shock, and Sophie's head pops into the attic from the ladder.

"Are you okay?" she asks, lightly growling, and all I can do is nod.

"A box fell on her foot, but her shifter healing is fixing it. Don't worry," Nath tells Sophie, smoothly lying, and I'm glad he did. Sophie wouldn't understand.

"You know how clumsy I can be," I mutter, my voice cracking a little. "Honestly, we are good." I manage to say much calmer.

"You are clumsy. Try not to drop something on yourself and scare me again, please," she sarcastically says and goes back down the ladder. I realise that I'm sitting directly on Nath's lap, and my head is rested on his chest, hearing his fast beating heart, and I swallow the nervous feeling which mixes in with how relaxed I am.

"What happened then?" Nath quietly asks, placing a finger under my chin, and lifting it so our faces are inches away and he can see me as I answer.

"Pain. It was like the time I got electrocuted by the toaster when I dropped a fork into it, but much worse," I explain, and he looks back at the crystals. "At least say you got some kind of idea about what it is?"

"I don't have a clue. The crystal was like nothing I've ever seen before, and it pushed me away when I tried to sense what it was," Nath admits, flashing his eyes at the bracelet. "I almost saw the start of an image locked in there, but the crystals are so strong, they threw me out."

"I think it's best we just leave it alone then. I don't want to do that again," I tell him.

"Neither do I," Nath mutters. "I am sorry I caused you any pain at all. I never knew that crystals could do that."

"It's not your fault," I reply, and I freeze as he presses a gentle kiss on my forehead.

"I'm not one to walk away from a puzzle. I will work out what it is, but not in a way that could hurt you. Don't worry," he whispers against my forehead, his warm breath is somewhat comforting.

"Why do you care?" I manage to reply, though my voice is almost silent.

"I don't think that is something even I know the answer to yet, beautiful...but I care, and I won't be going anywhere," he replies, and I gulp, staring at the insanely hot guy who just said he cares about me. "Now why don't we have a look around in these boxes and clean up some of these books?"

"Sounds perfect," I say with a nervous smile up at him, before climbing off his lap and getting to work.

CHAPTER
TWELVE

"That was a lot of work for pretty much nothing," I say, glancing at all the opened boxes and the dozens of weapons littering the attic floor. Nath stands with his hands on his hips, looking around all of the different things on the other side of the room. We only found two books in all the boxes, and a lot of it was just bubble wrap. I don't know what my mum expected me to do with all these weapons, but this clearly isn't giving me any answers.

"If anyone attacks you, you have a massive choice of weapons to use. Maybe your parents thought you might be in danger and they thought you'd need all this?" Nath asks, rubbing the back of his neck, and I swiftly look away from him before he sees the worry on my face. He could be onto something. Mum did say Frayan held death for me, that people died for me to be here and that some "she" would find me if I went back. Yet, it makes no sense. If mum wanted me to use these weapons, wouldn't she have trained me on how to use them at some point?

"I don't know how to use any of these things, so it is pointless. They are all made of crystals, and none of them look sharp enough to hurt anyone," I say, pointing at a bunch of them.

"It will take me a while to work out where these crystals come from and what we should do with them," Nath says, picking up a purple sword off the floor. The sword is made of what looks like amethyst, and it is very heavy, by the looks of it. I glance back at the dozens of daggers, arrows, knives, swords and there is even a whip, before picking the two books up off the ground and grabbing the one off the desk.

"I'm going to read all these and see if I can find anything useful in them," I tell Nath. "Thank you for helping me unpack all of this. Even if it was pointless."

"It's no problem. I am very interested in everything," he says, keeping his eyes on mine, and some part of me thinks he means me instead of the things in the room. I clear my throat and go to the ladder, knowing that falling for any of these guys would be dangerous. They are on a mission and pretending to be hunters. I am not in the right place to be thinking clearly about anything. I carefully climb down, balancing the books on each step above me before getting to the bottom and picking them off. I quickly run to my room and put them on the side, before going back into the corridor and watching as Nath pushes the ladder steps back and shuts the attic door.

"Are you going to be okay sleeping on the sofa? I have spare blankets and a pillow but no spare bed," I say. I would offer him my bed, but I'm a little selfish, and I just want to collapse into it tonight rather than the sofa.

"The sofa is perfect for me. I used to sleep in a sleeping bag in a tent for most my childhood, a sofa is a step up," he says, chuckling at my slightly shocked face, and he nods his head towards the stairs.

"Why did you sleep in a tent?"

"I'm a half breed, and until the war, we had to hide from not just humans but supernaturals. Mum did the best she could, but we moved a lot. Stayed in camping villages a lot," he says, and I step closer, placing my hand on his arm as I feel the urge to comfort him.

"I am sorry that was your upbringing. I mean, if you don't mind there being pillows between us, you can sleep in my bed?" I suggest.

"Are you suggesting we sleep together, Adie? I didn't know how much of a bad girl you are," Nath says, reaching closer and tucking a strand of my hair behind my ear as I try not to blush. "As much as sleeping next to you is appealing, I think a date first is a good idea. So, for now, it's the sofa."

"Okay," I say, squashing how disappointed I feel as I lower my hand away. Why the hell am I disappointed?

"Is that a yes then?"

"Yes, to what?" I ask, confused.

"A date of course," Nath asks. "I'm thinking I know the perfect place to take you."

"Okay," I reply, trying not to stumble on my words as he smiles, looking pleased.

"Good, I look forward to it," he winks. "As for tonight, I'm going to cook us all dinner. Are paprika burgers okay? I love them and bought you all the stuff to make them at the shops," he asks, changing the subject, but I just about hear what he says as I'm still focused on the fact one of the hottest guys I've ever met just asked me out on a date.

"You made lunch, I should make dinner," I reply.

"Let me. I love to cook. We didn't have much food growing up, and now I can have any food I like. I love to cook different things," he tells me.

"Then sure," I say, smiling and biting down on my bottom lip. Nath follows the movement, his eyes locked on my lip until I let it go, and he clears his throat.

"Before I start dinner, I want you and Sophie to put the bracelets on. I think they should be done now," he says, seeming a little dazed by something.

"Alright, where are they?" I ask.

"In the lounge," he tells me and nods his head towards the stairs. I follow him downstairs and into the lounge where there are two boxes on the coffee table, next to the bag Nath brought with him to the house. Nath sits on the sofa, right on the edge and opens the first box. A bright red light shines out of the box, making me look away until it dies down, and when I look back, Nath is floating a red gemstone bracelet in the air above his hand. There are six red stones, encased in a thin gold bracelet, and it looks like a normal piece of jewelry, a very stunning and expensive one.

"Come here, beautiful," Nath says, and I walk over, sitting on the sofa next to him. I hold my hands out, and he floats the bracelet into my open hands.

"I chose right picking rubies yesterday when I made this. It will match your other bracelet."

"You made this?"

"Yeah...it will go well with your ruby red hair," he says, picking the bracelet up out of my hand, and I hold my wrist out for him to clip it on next to my other one. They almost complement each other.

"Thank you doesn't seem enough for such a lovely gift," I tell him.

"It's nothing," he says, picking the other box up off the table before getting up. "I made a yellow topaz one for Sophie. Yellow is a happy colour, and it might cheer her up." Nath winks at me as I laugh, before walking out the room with the box in search for my sister. I rub my fingers over the new bracelet and smile to myself. *I have a date with Nath the hottie.*

CHAPTER THIRTEEN

The Frayan courts' royals decided to meet every four years when the three suns and moons would meet in the sky, and this day was known as the royal equinox. The queens and kings would dance, drink and eat together to show that Frayan would always be united. This was the way for thousands of years until one of the equinoxes went horribly wrong. No one knows the reason for the fall out on that destructive night, but war was called between the courts. Tall walls were built over the next months, cutting off all the courts of Frayan from each other. Peace was lost, and the royals were locked away for their own safety in each of their courts. This caused many problems within each court, and many, many deaths.

Queen Lilyanne of the Summer court was born two

hundred years after the war started, and the prophecy was written...

T pause, rubbing at the bottom of the page, but the ink is all smudged and unreadable. I sigh, closing the book and deciding it's best I try to read more of it tonight. So far, it just seems like a fairy tale. I learnt that the courts all made different things and loved to trade all their special goods. That the Summer court is on the beaches, made of sand and waves. The Winter court is in the mountains, made of snow and harsh weather. The Spring court is in the woods, their homes made high in the trees. The Autumn court kept my attention the most. The book explains the Autumn court is ever changing, made of all weather types. The people's homes are made in caves, inside what was described as a massive diamond crystal. The clear, shiny walls of the diamond reflect all the weather patterns and shine different lights onto the city throughout the year. I almost wish I could see that court, but I know that is impossible. I shake my head and grab my clothes, heading for the bathroom to get changed. I roughly pull my clothes on and start brushing my messy hair after pulling it out of the plait I had it in.

"Adie, there is someone at the door for you!" Sophie shouts up the stairs as I finish brushing my hair in the bathroom. I quickly pull up my black skirt over my hips and tuck in my white shirt. I know one of the guys is taking me to the base today, and I thought I might as well dress the part of receptionist. I slide the black heels on and glance at myself in the mirror. My red hair is in curls over my shoulders, parted in the middle, and I have put a little makeup on that somehow makes my eyelashes seem really long. The white shirt has little heart-shaped black buttons, which I've left the top two undone, as it looks good. *I can do this.* It's only a tour of the Hunter's Organisation base. Likely the deadliest place in the world for someone like me. *No big deal.*

"Adie!" Sophie shouts, before banging on the bathroom door. I grab my phone off the side cabinet and open the door, seeing my sister with her arms crossed. "The guy is downstairs with Nath, and I'm going to repack my stuff for the move to the castle."

"Alright, sis," I say, shutting the bathroom door as she goes to her room. I walk down the stairs, following the deep voices to the lounge, and I go to open the door when I hear my name and pause.

"What the fuck do you mean you are going on a date with Adie?" the man asks, and it takes me a few seconds to realise it's that Mich guy.

"What I just said. I'm not going to apologise for asking her or pull out of it. I like her," Nath states, making me smile a little. "Since when do you give a shit who I date? Who anyone dates? You don't date anyone, Mich, ever."

"I give a shit because we are on a fucking mission, and she is clearly becoming a big distraction," Mich snaps, though I can scent a lie on his lips. I frown, wondering what his real problem is because he is lying to Nath right now.

"I can do my job and date her," Nath replies.

"This is a mistake. Rick is seriously protective of her, there is no way he isn't going to lose his shit with you when you tell him," Mich snaps, and I frown. *Why would Rick be protective of me?*

"Rick will understand, and no doubt ask Adie out himself. I'm not selfish enough to stop them when I see the connection too," Nath retorts. My eyes widen when I realise he is talking about me dating both of them. Is that even a thing? Don't guys get jealous, or have I missed something by not dating? Is this normal now? I shake my head. I don't know a damn thing about guys. Maybe supernatural ones have different rules or something. I'm not sure I could even handle one guy, let alone two.

"You guys have all lost your goddamn minds over the pretty red head," Mich mutters, sounding more pissed off. I decide it might be a good time to walk in and stop this. I push the door open and walk in, seeing both the guys standing by the window, turning to look at me. Mich has a white shirt on, tucked into tight black trousers that showcase his small, toned waist that goes up to his large shoulders that the white shirt just about manages to keep in. Mich looks ready for work—and modeling for an office magazine. I have a sinking feeling I might be spending the day with him instead of Rick or Nath like I hoped. Nath's eyes seem to eat up my appearance, running over my dress and all the way up until he gets to my eyes. I briefly notice Mich looking at me strangely for a second before his emotions are blanked, and he is back to an emotionless expression.

"Hey, Mich," I awkwardly say, and smile at Nath as I've already seen him this morning when I made him breakfast as a thank you for dinner.

"Adelaide," he responds coldly. "I am taking you into the base today. I'm the safest as I can simply move us out of there if anything is wrong. We don't suspect Graves knows what you are, but it's better to be safe in these kinds of instances."

"Right, makes sense," I reply, and there's an awkward silence as Nath and Mich stare at each other for a little while before Nath walks over to me, pulling me into a tight hug. I didn't know we hugged now, but I don't pull away as he smells amazing this close. Like lemon and honey, I think. Whatever it is, my wolf is basically wanting to roll in it, and I'm not disagreeing with her as I press my head into his neck.

"Be safe today, and Mich isn't always a dickhead like he is acting like right now. Control issues," Nath whispers to me, but he purposely keeps his voice a little louder than he should do.

"I'm not a dickhead, wanker," Mich grumbles as Nath lets me go, winking at me before sliding around me to the door.

"I will look after Sophie today, at least until you are home, and then Mich is staying for tonight's watch," Nath explains to me. "The sofa is pretty comfy to be honest."

"I'm sure it won't be," Mich grumbles behind me. Wow, this guy is moodier than I thought.

"Oh, okay. Thank you for protecting me last

night, and I'm glad the sofa wasn't too bad," I say to Nath.

"Anything for you," he says, flashing me a seductive smile that makes my knees feel weak. "I'll literally do anything for you, or to you, my beautiful Adelaide."

"Enough of the flirty crap. Let's go, we don't have all day," Mich says, making me jump as my cheeks burn red, and Nath walks out the room, chuckling low. Mich storms past me, and I quickly follow him out of my house and towards his driveway. Mich unlocks the black Jeep, which I'm not surprised is his car because it's the most sensible. I'm getting the feeling Mich is the sensible one of the bunch. I quickly get into the passenger seat after struggling a little to climb in with the heels. I slide my phone into the side door as Mich turns the engine on and speeds out of the driveway. I struggle to clip my seatbelt in and notice Mich hasn't put his on at all.

"You should put your seatbelt on," I inform him.

"I can disappear anytime I want. If the car crashed, I would just leave. A seatbelt is pointless for someone like me," he explains, making it sound like that was obvious and I'm stupid for not realising it. I really don't like this guy.

"Are you always a dickhead?" I blurt out. "I can see why you and Josh are friends."

"I'm not like Josh," he replies sharply, looking at me for a second with his eyes narrowed. "You don't know any of us to judge us this quickly, Adelaide."

"You sure do act like it, Mich," I respond. "If you don't want me to see you as a complete asshole, try being nicer."

"Why would I care what you see me as?" he asks, and I don't answer him, choosing to look out the window instead. He is right, he doesn't have to care what I think, and he clearly doesn't. The man just frustrates me.

"You worry me. I like to keep my pack in control. I'm the beta, the one that solves the problems and deals with anything that threatens us," Mich randomly says, his voice quiet like he doesn't want to tell me this, but some part of him feels like he needs to. He says he doesn't care about my opinion, but here he is, telling me something to change it. *Damn confusing man.*

"You think I threaten the guys?" I ask, assuming he is talking about me. I really don't think I threaten them in any kind of way. They are all built like gods, and they can clearly protect themselves. *How could I threaten them in any kind of way?*

"Simply, yes. Rick and Nath are going to argue over you because they are both falling fast. Josh is one stone's throw away from losing his shit and doesn't need any changes in this mission. Nath already won't listen to my advice," Mich says. "I could keep listing the shit that has changed in a week, but I think you get the gist."

"Maybe some changes are good?" I suggest lightly. "Maybe you don't always need to be in complete control."

"Maybe not, and then maybe we all get killed protecting you, Adie," Mich mutters, turning down a road that seems to appear out of nowhere in a row of trees. The road seems to stretch on forever, and in the silent car, it soon becomes uncomfortable.

"I won't get everyone killed," I tell him. "I'm only here for a month, Mich."

"I owe Rick, Nath and Josh big time. I wouldn't be the man I am without them, and this isn't just about control like you are thinking. They are my family, and I won't let anyone break that," he tells me, glancing at me for a second as his hands tighten on the wheel.

"How do you think you owe them?" I ask, wondering if he will open up to me and hoping to distract him from thinking I'm the wolf in the pigs'

126

pen. *I mean I am a wolf, but I'm not going to kill everyone.*

"When I was a kid, I lost my hearing when my pack was attacked and witches cut my ears off when I was in wolf form. I was lucky to survive when the rest of my pack was killed, but I was too scared to talk to anyone, and I couldn't hear a thing for a long time. Another pack adopted me from the human social care system and brought me up. I had always been able to speak in people's heads, because I'm half witch, and I decided to use that even though my hearing healed over time. I wasn't brave enough to admit that I didn't know how to speak and ask for help. Rick, Josh and Nath spent months teaching me in secret, so I wouldn't be embarrassed," he explains, glancing at me with those deep brown eyes of his.

"That's so sweet of them," I say, seeing the guys in a different light. *Especially Josh.* I never thought in a million years a guy like him would do that for anyone.

"They are my pack, and Rick is our alpha. I don't know what it is about you, but you are different," he tells me. "I just hope different doesn't destroy us like I believe it would. I bet half the pack wouldn't even fight being destroyed for you."

"What does that even mean?" I ask.

"Doesn't matter, Adie. Here we are," Mich nods his head in front of us, and I follow his movement to see the massive electric fence gate we are driving up to. There are three gates, each one lined with men in dark suits, only the yellow dragon symbol of the Hunter's Organisation on their uniforms. They have guns held at their sides. "Time to enter hell. You best smile."

CHAPTER
FOURTEEN

"**Y**ou are clear to enter," the hunter says through Mich's window, and pats the side of the car before Mich drives us through the three gates as they slowly open one by one.

"Don't look so nervous," Mich says, and I flash him a glare. "See, that's a better expression."

"There I thought the dickhead side of you was gone for a bit," I mutter, and he only laughs as he drives us down the gravel driveway. I'm surprised that the hunter base is such a small building, with five windows and only one level by the looks of it. There are dozens of cars parked outside in the parking lot so it takes Mich a few minutes to find an empty spot and park up.

"It's smaller than I thought it would be," I admit,

needing to speak as the nervous tension flittering through me is overwhelming.

"You shouldn't judge a book by its cover," Mich warns, and then he gets out of the car. I undo my seatbelt and slide out, shutting the door before Mich locks it as he comes around the car to my side. We walk out of the cars to the main path and up to the building which has sliding glass doors that open automatically when we get close. The inside is one big room with a row of five elevators on the one wall. The walls are painted a gold fancy colour which matches the golden tiled floor in the room that shines under the bright lights. There is a big receptionist desk which is empty of anyone behind it, and there is a phone ringing out. It is creepy how the entire room is empty. There are lovely flowers in large vases all around the room and on the desk, and paintings of beaches on the walls. You would never expect this place kills supernaturals for a living. You'd never expect this place is full of horrors.

I swallow the nervous feeling in my throat as I look around and tell myself that Mich would get me out of here if there is an issue. I expected it to be full of guards, but when I look around more closely, I can see the cameras everywhere and the no doubt hidden security. Mich nods his head to the elevators, and we walk over, going to the one on the far right. Mich presses the button for the elevators, and we wait quietly for them to come down. A few minutes later, it beeps and the doors open to reveal the empty, gold elevator with shiny gold coloured metal walls. We get inside, and there is only one button which says "BOSS" in bold white letters on a black background. Mich presses that button, which lights up red, and the doors close. There is a tense silence as we wait for the elevator to go down, neither one of us wanting to say anything, and I get more nervous by the second. I nearly jump when I hear Mich's voice in my head, sounding like a whisper.

I will keep you safe. Breathe, Adie. I look up at him, and he nods once at me, his strong, determined eyes making me realise I need to relax and let out the breath I am holding. It seems like forever before the elevator stops, and the doors slowly open again. Mich walks out first, and I follow, pausing to look around the new room we have come into. This room is just as nice as the reception room, but more personal and feels like a room in someone's house with its dark red and brown painted walls and wooden floors. It's almost homey. There are filing cabinets lining two walls, locked tight, and bookcases filled with old books on the one wall. It seems a bit odd to have a room like this in a hunter's base, but I am pretty sure this is an office as there is a desk in the middle. There are two laptops on top of the desk, new expensive looking ones, and a few jars filled with pink glitter looking stuff next to a desk lamp. I will have to ask the others what that stuff is later.

One of the bookcases moves, opening up, and Mr. Graves walks in, clicking his walking stick against the wood floor as the door closes behind him. Even for an evil place, that is one cool door. Mr. Graves's whole face lights up in a big smile when he sees Mich and me, and he walks over to us, his eyes drifting over my outfit in a way that feels creepy.

"I am so happy to see you here, Adelaide," he states. "Looking more beautiful than the last time we met."

If he keeps looking at you like his next meal, I'm going to break his face and screw this mission up. Mich whispers in my head, and I have to clear my throat, trying to pretend I didn't just hear him say that to me. *Since when was Mich protective?*

"I can't wait to see around. It's not every day you get invited into one of the legendary hunter's bases," I say, putting on the fakest happy voice I can and hiding how terrified I am in it. I'm not lying when I say they are legendary, but not in a good way. They are legendary because most people are scared of hunters and stay well out of their way.

"Legendary you say? Well, I suppose we are. Everything we do is for the best of the human species! We will be remembered in history as legendary," he says, sounding completely crazy. I suppose he would have to tell himself something so he could sleep at night.

"I agree. That is why I have decided to accept your job proposal," I say before he can say anything else. We might as well get this out of the way, so I can get the hell out of here for today.

"Brilliant. Well, this day just keeps getting better and better," Mr. Graves says, holding out a hand for me to shake. I shake his cold hand, feeling like I've just struck a deal with the devil, before dropping it as quickly as I can. I glance up at Mich, who doesn't look impressed as he watches me with his arms crossed.

"Why don't I give Adie a tour, Graves?" Mich suggests. "I remember you saying you have meetings all day or I would suggest you come with us."

"Yes, that sounds like a brilliant idea. I only wish for Adie to visit the reception, this floor, and floor three. The others aren't for her to see," Mr. Graves says, walking away from us and going to sit on his desk, resting his walking stick against the desk.

"Yes, sir," Mich replies, nodding his head at the elevator for me to follow him.

"Why not?" I blurt out to Mr. Graves.

Adie, for god's sake, don't ask questions you don't want to know the answers to. You know why he doesn't want you to see the other floors. They torture our people on those floors. Mich whispers in my mind as I stare at Mr. Graves and keep my expression as natural as possible as I regret saying a word now. Of course, Mr. Graves wouldn't want me to see those floors, they must scare anyone.

"A creature as lovely as you doesn't need to see the monsters we have to keep here. It is for your own good," Mr. Graves smoothly answers.

"Okay. I understand completely," I whisper, not wanting to see that anyway. I know I would just want to break them all out, and knowing I couldn't would haunt me. I have to remember that the end plan is to get them all out, and that's what will happen if I just play the receptionist game well. That is what the guys are here for. They are the heroes, and I'm like their temporary sidekick.

"Please start next Monday, and I will get your ID

ADELAIDE'S FATE

passes done in time," Mr. Graves says, and I smile at him.

"I can't wait. Goodbye for now, Mr. Graves," I reply with another fake smile and turn around with Mich, who presses the button for the elevator. We both get in, and Mr. Graves's eyes stay locked on mine until the elevator doors close.

"You did good," Mich whispers, his voice almost silent, and I turn, looking up at him, and nod once. I'm almost thankful he used his real voice and didn't speak in my mind. His voice is comforting. Mich quickly shows me around level three, which is filled with coffee machines, microwaves on counters and fridges. It is clearly the break room, and I can see why Mr. Graves wouldn't mind me coming in here. When we have seen that, Mich leads me back to the car, and I quickly get inside, shutting the door and putting my seatbelt on as Mich starts the car.

"One month," I mutter to myself, needing to hear it out loud and forgetting that Mich is even there for a moment.

"Yes. It seems like he only wants you for a pretty decoration piece in his reception. You literally have to smile with those pretty lips for a month, and then you can be free," Mich says, placing his hand on my arm for a moment. The contact seems to calm me, because I find myself smiling at him.

"Pretty lips, huh? Is that almost a compliment?" I ask and quickly glance at Mich as he laughs loudly, and I can't help but laugh with him.

"Yeah, maybe it was," he says, and I rest my head back, still chuckling as I roll my eyes at him. *Maybe Mich isn't as bad as I thought.*

FIFTEEN

"Thanks for today, Mich," I say walking up my driveway next to his side, briefly sneaking glances at him. Mich glimpses down at me as he slides his keys into his pocket, a frown back on his face.

"You did well. I'm impressed," he mutters. "I was sure I would have to save your ass, but that didn't happen."

"Adie!" I hear Rick shout before I can reply to Mich. I turn to see Rick walking out of his door and over to us. Mich and I wait for Rick to jog over to us, and he pulls me into a tight hug the moment he gets close. *Do Nath and Rick like to hug all the time? When did I get so lucky?* I don't know if it is a shifter thing to hug when we see each other, but I do like it as I press my head into his chest and he holds me tighter. My wolf suddenly pushes into my mind, wanting me to shift, and I have to stop her, making her calm down so I can breathe in Rick's musky peppermint scent. *Hot wolf guys hugging you should be a shifter rule or something.*

"How was it?" Rick asks, pulling back from me, but keeping his warm hands on my shoulders, rubbing his thumbs in circles.

"Good as it could have been. I start next week," I tell him, trying to hide how nervous I am.

"Adie has a good poker face, that's for sure," Mich says. "Is Nath still at hers?"

"No, he is around ours with Sophie. They are playing some game on the PS4," Rick replies, "and Sophie is apparently some kind of queen at those games and is beating him."

"Nath must be Sophie's new best friend, she loves playing those games," I reply, grinning up at Rick.

"So does Nath," Rick replies. "I actually wondered if you would come back to mine. Tay wants to say sorry for the crazy way she reacted when you met."

"Is the sorry going to be real, or she is going to throw things at me again?" I ask. "As I want to get something to defend myself with if she is going to do that."

"It's real. Tay is just protective of us, and I really feel she is sorry. You might not have seen her, but she was flying around your house last night and kept checking in on you," Rick explains to me.

"Rick means she sees us all as her family, and you are a threat, and she wants to keep an eye on you," Mich says with a chuckle as my eyes widen, and he heads towards the house.

"Look, I won't let her throw things at you. Just come over?" Rick asks, slowly lowering his hands down my arms. I nod with a sigh, and he grins before turning to walk towards his home. I follow him, praying the pixie isn't going to throw anything else at me, and if she does, I'm hiding behind Rick. He can get hit by flying shit instead for guilt tripping me into coming over.

"Where is Tay from?" I ask, curious about her.

"The hunter base, actually. We rescued her on one of our first days, and everyone thinks she just escaped," Rick says. "Tay was pretty sick for about a month, and we were lucky she made it."

"I'm sorry she was ill. Does she talk about where she was from before the base? I didn't know pixies where even real," I ask. "I've seen videos on the internet of little blue demon things that like to cause trouble. They like to steal drinks and shiny things, but they don't look like Tay. Tay looks like a pink version of Tinkerbell, with a bigger attitude problem."

"Tay doesn't talk, well, not any language we can understand. She just nods her head to say yes or no, or points at things. She can't tell us where she is from," Rick replies, and I think back to when I met her. She could definitely talk.

"She does talk. I remember her very clearly telling me to 'go' when she was throwing things at me," I tell him.

"You can understand her? That language she speaks?" Rick asks, stopping in his tracks in shock for a moment before he keeps walking to the door which Mich has left open.

"Yes..." I drawl.

"That's insane. How is it possible only you hear her?" he asks, and I shrug. *I don't have a clue.* The only thing I can think of is that Tay might be from Frayan and that's why I can understand her. *But then why can't Nath?*

"Maybe I could ask her where she is from?" I suggest, stepping in the house behind Rick, and shutting the door behind me. Rick watches me, running a hand through his hair as he thinks about it.

"I don't know...she doesn't trust people, and even if you can talk to her, I doubt she will tell you anything. It took me all day to get her to agree to say sorry," he says and sighs. "Though it wouldn't hurt to ask. Maybe we might be able to find her real home and take her back somehow."

"I did get the feeling she doesn't like me," I chuckle, and Rick smirks.

"I think everyone likes you, and you just don't realise the reason why," he cryptically replies. I hear Sophie's laugh float over to us, and I walk further into the room to see Sophie sitting on the couch next to Nath, and she has her hands in the air.

"You lose again, sucker!" she cheers for herself. She always was a sore winner.

"You cheated!" Nath protests.

"Hey, guys!" I interrupt, and they both wave at me before going back to their game.

"Another game? And no goddamn cheating, kid!" Nath demands, and I shake my head as they start up a new game. *Someone's a little competitive.*

"Nath can't stand to lose, so Sophie will have to let him win soon to be able to go home," Rick whispers to me, and I laugh quietly. "Let's go to my room, Tay is up there."

"Alright," I reply, pulling my eyes away from Nath and Sophie. Rick offers me his hand when I face him, and I surprise myself by sliding my hand into his without a single pause. Rick leads me up the stairs and back to his room, pushing the door open and closing it behind me. Tay is sat on his pillow, her arms crossed in annoyance, and she downright glares at me. The pixie looks cuter than ever with her pink hair almost floating around her, and her little wings fluttering as she watches me. Though I now know cute means evil, so I keep myself just behind Rick.

"Time to say sorry," Rick demands, letting go of my hand and crossing his arms as he stares at Tay. When he tries to step closer, I move myself behind him and he looks back at me, shaking his head at my hiding. *I don't care though, that pixie is evil.* "Adie is sticking around, so you need to behave and be nice to her."

"She must go," Tay mutters in an overly sweet voice, locking her eyes with me. I feel like I'm her prey when she does that, and it's seriously creepy. I know that little pixie is thinking of ways to kill me. I can see it in her damn spectacular pink eyes.

"Did she say sorry?" Rick turns his head to look at me as he asks, and I shake my head.

"Not exactly," I dryly reply.

"Tay..." Rick warns, raising his eyebrows at her, and they have a staring contest. How is he not scared of her? "Tay, I swear I will hide that pink pillow you like to sleep on, and I won't buy you anymore pink bath bombs if you don't say sorry." I smile at Rick's parent attitude and how Tay lets out a long sigh before flying up and coming straight towards me. I resist the urge to run away as she flies in the air right in front of me, sits on the edge of Rick's shoulder and looks down at my hand on Rick's arm. I get the impression she wants me to remove my hand, but I don't, and she rolls her pretty eyes at me.

"I am sorry for the throwing, but you must go home. To Frayan. Not here," she says, and I frown. "The fates are calling you."

"Why do I need to go there?" I ask and lower my voice as Rick looks over his shoulder in confusion. "I can't go there."

"Your people need you. All dead without you. You are selfish to stay here," she mutters, judging me for something I have no clue what she is going on about.

"My people?" I ask her, hoping she will explain whatever she clearly knows.

"Fray...yours. Fate calls you," she says, her tone suggesting that should make perfect sense to me.

"You aren't making much sense, little pixie," I reply, letting go of Rick and putting my hands on my hips.

"You are stupid. Why does fate pick a stupid girl like you?" she huffs and shakes her head at me.

"Who the hell are you calling stupid?" I ask as Tay flies around me to the open window.

"Next time, I will throw harder and hit your head. Then you might finally understand," Tay grumbles before transforming into an owl and flying away out the window.

"What did she say? What are your people and where does she think you need to go?" Rick rapidly asks, and I drop my hands from my hips, and I rub my face from the stress.

"It's complicated," I mutter. "Though I didn't get a chance to ask her where she is from, I think I have an idea." The way Tay talked about Frayan, where fairies are meant to live, I believe she is from there. It would explain everything. I don't have a clue what she is talking about with fate and all that.

"Meaning you don't want to tell me?" Rick asks, sounding a little hurt as I look up at him.

"Rick, we have only just met. Why would I trust you with all my secrets?" I ask, feeling frustrated, and freeze when Rick stares down at me in a way I don't really understand. Rick lifts a hand, drifting his fingers down my cheek and to my neck.

"Don't you feel it?" he asks, and I gulp as his hand goes to the back of my neck, and he steps closer, so our bodies are brushed against each other. "Can't you feel what I might be to you?"

"No," I whisper.

"Then maybe this will help you realise and trust me, because I'm not going anywhere," he whispers before pulling me into a scorching kiss. It's the kind of kiss that no one could ever forget, and every natural instinct in me tells me never to let him go. My hands slide into his soft hair as he pulls me closer, tilting my head to the side a little as he deepens the kiss. I feel completely in his control with every movement, and all I can do is submit to him as he steals my breath with the passionate kiss.

"Rick! Come here!" Rick pulls away from me at the sound of someone shouting, resting his forehead against mine as we both breathe heavily. "Rick, man, get down here!" I recognise the voice as Mich, and the annoyance flashing across Rick's face is cute as we stare at each other.

"I will be right back," Rick mutters. "I need to tell you something, and we never get a chance to be alone."

"Okay," I shakily say, and he reluctantly pulls away from me, walking to the door and leaving it open as he walks out. I wait still and silently for a while before I get bored and decide to wander. I walk around Rick's room and go to the dresser by the door, smiling at the strange collection of Harry Potter things on the side. There is everything from the DVD collection to a toy wand that looks way too real. Seems Rick likes Harry Potter, which is so damn cool. I run my finger over the wand and a deep voice from right behind me makes me jump.

"You shouldn't look through people's shit that isn't yours," Josh grumbles, his voice deep and threatening.

"Hello, Josh, lovely to see you too. Hasn't anyone ever told you it's rude to sneak up on someone?" I mutter, turning to face him with my arms crossed. "What do you want?"

"I can't find any record of your parents, or you. Not even Sophie. I found your parents' death records, but that's it." He pauses. "Why are you so hidden, *sweetheart?*" he asks me.

"I didn't know I was," I reply, stepping back as he laughs, a sarcastic and cruel laugh.

"You're almost as much as a ghost as we all are," Josh growls as he steps closer, hunting me with every step. "Now tell me what I want to know. Being pretty isn't going to win me over like it did my friends."

"I don't know why my parents kept us hidden. I've already told you this, Josh. Why are you so determined to make me out to be the bad guy?" I ask. "Because that is what you have treated me as since I got here."

"No, hidden is one thing and understandable in this world, but you are a ghost. Sweetheart, there is no record of your birth, no record of your sister's, and there is nothing. You said you went to university, but I can't find any proof of that," Josh growls. "So, something isn't adding up, and I want to know what you are hiding."

"I had fake ID for university, for all my schools," I tell him. "It was safer that way."

"And where the hell did your parents get that from? How did your parents, who by the looks of it were poor as fuck, manage to afford to make you all that shit?" Josh asks, stepping closer to me with every few words until he's pressed right up to my chest. I stare up at him, holding his gaze and refusing to back down. I haven't done anything wrong, and I'm goddamn tired of this guy hating me for no reason.

"That's enough." I flinch at Rick's protective growl from the door. "Get the fuck away from her if you're going to be a dick."

"I'm not asking you to trust me, Josh. I don't know all my parents' secrets. They died before I got a chance to find out. If you don't remember, I told you all that. I've been nothing but honest with you all, and yet there is so much you lot are keeping from me. I don't even know what you are, Josh, so don't you dare be a shithead to me for things I don't know," I angrily reply, poking my finger into his chest before pushing past him. I pass Rick by the door, and he gently grabs my arm, stopping me leaving.

"I always find out everything," Josh darkly responds just behind us, and Rick looks away from me, glaring at him.

"Good luck with that, Josh," I mutter, turning to look at Josh myself, smiling before walking out the door as Rick lets me go. Rick catches up to me in the corridor, gently grabbing my arm again, and this time turns me to look at him.

"I'm sorry about Josh. Can we have that talk later? It can wait. I need to talk to him," Rick says. "He is like a brother to me, and I need to explain some things."

"Sure," I say, placing my hand over his for a second before he lets me go and walks back to his room, slamming the door behind him. As I walk down the stairs, I hear a big smash and the loud bangs of them likely fighting, and I wonder if I should help. *Ah well, they are supernaturals and they will heal.* I get to the bottom of the stairs and walk over to Nath and Sophie who don't even pause their games at the noises. I sit right in the middle of them as they finish another racing game, and Sophie wins in her pink car.

"You suck," Sophie tells Nath, and there's another loud smash upstairs, drawing her eyes to the ceiling as a little dust falls from it. "Shouldn't someone go and check that out?"

"Nope. Rick and Josh always fight. Don't worry, we heal quickly, remember? Wanna play, Adie?" Nath asks and pulls a spare controller off the coffee table. He doesn't even seem to react at all to his friends fighting. It really must be a normal thing for them.

"Sure," I shrug.

"Now you're going to lose to two girls," Sophie grins and winks at me as Nath groans.

"When did girls get so good at racing games?" he asks. "I've never met anyone that can beat me, and a damn fifteen-year-old did."

"Since forever. Games aren't just for guys anymore," I say with a laugh. *Girls can do anything we want. It's clear Nath is going to learn that as we beat his ass on this game.*

CHAPTER
SIXTEEN

"You will look after her, won't you?" I ask the Scottish woman, Rick's great-aunt Lucinda, before she reassured me, one more time. I'm sure she is getting annoyed with me at this point, but I can't help but panic. Sophie is the last of my family, and she is so young. She is my responsibility, and if I make the wrong choice, she suffers, which I can't let happen. Lucinda sighs, tilting her head to the side as her eyes run over me from head to toe. I briefly glance over at Sophie who is picking up her rucksack after the four wolves that came with this woman finished packing her boxes into their truck. Sophie hasn't taken all her things, only what she thinks she will need for now, and I know we can come back for the other things eventually.

"Lass, we will look after her like she is family. You need to be stronger than this and trust your pack. They need you brave," she says, placing her hand on my arm in a comforting way and lowering her voice. "We know you are risking your life staying here for a month to help the boys. That debt will be repaid, and looking after your sister is a given, Adie. I didn't miss the overprotective way Rick spoke of you, and he needs a strong mate." My eyes widen at the suggestion of mating with Rick. That's a big thing, and we are nowhere near that. I doubt he even likes me that much. Since our kiss last week, he has avoided me and made sure that he wasn't the one staying over to protect us. I've been stuck three nights with grumpy Josh who wouldn't talk to me as he stayed. I don't know what happened between Josh and Rick, but they clearly made some agreement to avoid me. Mich and Nath are different though. Our nights are usually fun, and I enjoy learning about them and where they grew up.

"Sophie has been through a lot. This isn't about me being brave, it is about me not wanting to mess her up," I quietly reply.

"One thing I know how to deal with is kids that

have had to grow up far more quickly than they should. I have this handled, lass," she tells me, but I know I still look worried as she keeps talking. "Trust me, this is what is best for her." I nod once, knowing she is right before she goes to the door, stopping next to Sophie.

"We will wait in the truck for you. Say goodbye, Sophie," she tells her kindly, and Sophie gives her a shaky nod. Sophie looks over at me with tear-streaked cheeks and nervous eyes.

"Come here," I say, opening my arms at the same time for Sophie, and she runs into them, squeezing her arms tight around my waist.

"I don't want to go," she admits in a whisper that is meant for only me to hear. "I feel like I'm never going to see you again."

"You will, stop worrying. You are my sister, Sophie. You can do this," I pull her out the hug and hold my hands on her shoulder, keeping my voice firm even though I feel like crying.

"Will you be safe though?" she asks me. "If I lose you..."

"Of course I will be. I have the guys to keep me safe. You've spent the week with them like I have, and you know they will keep me safe," I remind her.

"They feel like family," she tells me quietly. "I think I'm going to miss them."

"Pack," I whisper. "Family is pack. It's something Nath said to me as he tried to explain what the others were to him."

"Family is pack. I like that saying," she says and chuckles low. "I best go. They said it's a long drive and we have to change cars a few times to make sure we aren't followed before the witches can take us to the castle."

"Go. Be brave, sis, and I love you. Remember, one month," I tell her, and she smiles at me as she pulls out of my arms.

"One month," she repeats, holding her head high and walking out of the house as I watch her go. I walk to stand by the door, watching as Sophie gets into the truck. She waves a hand at me before the door shuts, and the truck speeds out of the driveway. I silently watch the truck disappear into the shadows of the trees, hoping I did the right thing and knowing it's done now. It's not like I had much choice anyway. I have to keep her safe. I close the door and rest my head against it, knowing it will only be an hour until the guys get back from their mission tonight, and I won't be alone again. The distraction to get Sophie out was planned well to make sure no one was watching the guys or me. I run up to my room and grab one of the Fray books, before sitting on my bed and opening it to the page I got to last time. I might as well read to distract myself.

Prophecies are only made by gods or fates. This has been known for many years, as it is their curse to prophesy their family's future when usually the prophecy is never good or kind. The fates and gods have unlimited power, therefore they had to be given a downfall, and only if the prophecy is fulfilled can a fate help their family. One of the original fates married a queen of Frayan after returning from his time on Earth. The queen of the Autumn court and the fate were blessed with happiness, and on their wedding day, Queen Lilyanne was born to the Summer court.
The fate made the prophecy on that very night, which would in turn link his own child and Queen Lilyanne for a destructive war in the future. The words to the prophecy were told only to himself, the queen of the Autumn court and Queen Lilyanne when she was older, but there were many rumours of it foretelling a great war. Many years passed where nothing but peace graced Frayan, the rumours forgotten, and no child was born of

the mating between the fate and the queen of the Autumn court.

The day the fate announced a pregnancy, Queen Lilyanne was eighteen years old, and she killed her parents before declaring war on the entire Frayan world. One by one, the courts fell over the nine months, and Queen Lilyanne attacked the Autumn court, killing the fate, the queen of the Autumn court and her newborn child. The Frayan courts are no more, and Queen Lilyanne rules over all of Frayan.

Some Fray whisper that the baby was hidden on another world, kept safe, but there is no proof in the five years since Frayan fell to Queen Lilyanne's rule. If anyone is reading this book, I must have escaped and gotten this book somewhere safe. Someone must remember our history, even as Queen Lilyanne burns all knowledge and all books about it.

The Frayan courts and their royals must be remembered. May one day they return for vengeance.

I PAUSE and turn the page over, seeing a note stuck to the blank page. The note is written on my mum's flower paper, and I gently pull it off, before opening it up.

. . .

THE FRAY MAN who gave me this book died of old age shortly after we met. I searched for many years for this, and there are answers in here. You need to understand. This is everything you are looking for, my Adelaide. - Mum.

I SHAKE my head and flip through the rest of the book, where there is nothing but blank pages. So, there was a prophecy, an evil queen and rumours of a hidden child? I don't get the answers my mum is trying to tell me. I close the book and put my hands over the cover, the old brown leather which I think has little drops of blood all over it. Someone died to get this book to Earth safely. Why would the queen of Frayan want everything burnt? All the history gone? I shake my head, not having a single clue.

"How the hell is this book answers to anything?" I say to myself, putting it on the bed in frustration and standing up off the bed. I walk to the window, crossing my arms and staring out at the full moon in the sky. *If this was mum's way of getting me answers, I am never going to know who I am.*

SEVENTEEN

"Ready for your first day?" Josh sarcastically asks as he answers the front door and walks back into his house. "You might as well just walk in rather than knocking at this point."

"Where are the others?" I ask him, ignoring his sarcastic statement as he picks his leather jacket up off the hook and puts it on.

"There was an emergency mission last night, and they all got called in. Rick and Nath are still at work. Mich is in bed because he worked all day and night yesterday. So, I'm stuck with the awful job of taking you in today," he explains, and I roll my eyes at him.

"Are you always this dramatic?" I ask.

"Always," he grins, looking pleased with himself. I try to ignore how his messy black hair looks brushed today and ridiculously sexy. Everything about Josh screams sexy biker man. Which I may have gone through a phase of thinking it was the hottest thing ever.

"Let's just go," I mutter, turning around and walking to the car. Josh unlocks the red sportscar this time, and I quickly get in. I don't admit that the seats are extremely comfy or that this is the nicest car I have ever been in. I think it's an Audi, but I never cared much for car names. Josh gets in the driver seat and does his seatbelt up at the same time I do, our hands brushing against each other, and he glares at me.

"Do you think being mean and cruel is the best way to push everyone away?" I ask him, pulling my hand away and regretting saying it when he narrows his eyes at me before looking away and starting the car up. It starts to heavily rain as Josh pulls the car out of the driveway, and I'm almost thankful for the sound in the deadly silent car.

"Why do you think I push people away?" he asks.

"Because you're scared you will hurt them. It's easier to make them hate and be scared of you than

159

to admit you are afraid you will lose control of your-self," I blurt out. *Ah well, I've said it now.*

"You don't even know what I am, so what gives you the right to act like my therapist?" Josh snaps, and I turn in my seat, looking at him. He doesn't scare me like he should do, but I can see past the defensive, frightening attitude he puts up.

"I grew up with humans, and I pushed every one of them away that got close to me because I knew I could hurt them. I knew I wasn't safe to be around, and it's damn lonely to do it," I tell him. "You get angry with Rick, Nath and Mich because it doesn't work with them. They see past it, and you can't push them away. I can see past it too, and that's why you hate me."

"Sweetheart, you have no idea how dangerous and frightening I can be," he growls, tightening his hands on the steering wheel so tight that it leaves indents. "But I don't hate you."

"Yeah, I get that you can act like the big bad wolf, but I have a sneaking suspicion that you have no bite," I say, and he laughs, smirking at me.

"I have bite, sweetheart. I spend most of my every damn day keeping the side of me that would do more than bite under control," he admits to me.

"What are you? Other than dark angel?" I ask, curious.

"Do you even know what a dark angel can do?" he asks.

"Nope, why don't you tell me?" I reply, and he smirks at me before pulling the car over at the side of the road. I flash him a confused look as he turns to face me, reaching for my hand which I let him pick up. I gasp as he runs a finger over my wrist, a stinging pain being left in the place of where he touches, and he lifts my wrist up, kissing the spot. A wave of pleasure spirals through me, mixed with the tad bit of pain he left before.

"We can cause pain with our touch," he whispers seductively, "but I like a little bit of pain mixed in with my pleasure anyway."

"What else can you do?" I ask as he lets my hand go, and I clear my throat. Josh only smirks, clearly confident in the effect he has on me. I have no doubt he knows his way around women.

"I have some powers to see into people's past, but I've never been good at controlling that one," he remarks. I wonder for a second if he can get the answers to my past I need if the last two books my mum left me don't. Josh might be able to see my past, at least when I was born, and the answers I want from that. I don't know if he will help me, but it's worth a shot to ask.

"Josh—" I start to ask, but he cuts me off.

"I am also a half demon, and that demon side of me isn't under control yet," he says, and I remember that demons destroyed Paris. Killed all those humans and supernaturals. He is half demon.

"Demon?" I whisper, feeling frightened for only a second, and whatever Josh sees on my face makes him go cold. Josh turns away from me, but I know the damage has been done, he thinks I'm scared of him.

"I'm not scared," I tell him.

"You should be. My demon powers make me drain other people, especially supernaturals. You might want to ask the others what happened at the castle before this mission and why I am not welcome back there," he snaps. "Why you *should* be scared, Adelaide."

"Why don't you just tell me?" I ask.

"Because you are already scared of me...I don't need to bother pushing you away, you already look ready to run, sweetheart," he says and starts the car, making it clear this conversation is over. I silently sit back in my seat as he takes us to the hunter's base, and Josh hands over both our IDs to the hunters at the gates. After they have checked them, they let us in, and Josh hands me one of the small plastic cards. I accept it off him and see my name and a scanner number on the bottom of the card. There isn't anything else on it, but I doubt anyone can just walk into here. I am sure the cameras are checking the cars somehow.

"Remember, I am always near you, and you are safe. Even if you can't see me," Josh says, and I almost think he is being sweet before I shake my head and remember that this is Josh. Josh doesn't do sweet, but he does do confusing apparently. We both get out of the car, and Josh locks it before we walk up to the building. Mr. Graves is waiting for us in the reception room, and he smiles tightly when he sees us.

"Adelaide! Are you ready for your first day?" he asks, and I nod. "Josh, the command needs you downstairs on level five. I will find you after I show Adelaide what to do up here."

"Yes, sir," Josh nods, and he walks to the elevators. I almost panic for a second that he is leaving me alone in here when I remember his words in the car and see his dark eyes on me as the elevator doors shut. That look is full of confidence and protection. I can do this, and Josh will protect me if I can't.

"Come here," Mr. Graves kindly asks, snapping me out of it, and I plaster a fake smile on my face as he leads me into the receptionist counter. Mr. Graves shows me how to answer the phone and direct the phone calls to the right area before showing me the massive pile of paperwork that he wants sorted into a filing cabinet under the counter.

"Good luck, and if you need anything, hold the number one down on the phone, it will direct the phone call to me," he explains.

"Thank you."

"No, thank you. I hope I don't have to remind you not to wander around. This place is full of very dangerous people, and remember, you are always being watched," he says, nodding his head at one of the cameras in the corner of the room which is pointed at me.

"I have no plans to go anywhere but this desk, your office if you call me, and the break room to get myself a coffee later."

"Brilliant. This week, I need you here through Wednesday, and the rest of the week you can have off on me," he explains.

"Thank you," I reply with a smile.

"I'm sure this is going to work out well for us all," he says, patting my shoulder gently, and I pull my shoulder away without thinking. He doesn't say anything, but I see the annoyance flash in his eyes before he walks to the elevator and gets in. I quickly look away as the phone rings, and I answer it, directing the phone call to the right department, and try to pretend that I'm working a normal job. *It's only one month, Adie. One month.*

EIGHTEEN

"Popcorn, chocolate, friends, wine and my choice of movie. This is a perfect reward for my first week at work," I say to Nath who grins as I take the bowl of popcorn off him and put my wine on the side table next to my chocolate. Josh and Rick are sat on the floor, resting their backs on the sofa. I look over at Mich on the other sofa, laying down with his legs crossed, and Tay who is sitting on the coffee table with her own collection of food. Pack is family. I don't know who suggested movie night, but somehow, we all ended up here, and they let me choose a movie. I chose the latest Marvel film because you can never go wrong with one of their movies. They are amazing. Mich presses play with the remote, and I rest my head on Nath's shoulder as I watch the film. His hand somehow gets to resting on my knee, and Rick moves closer, until his shoulder is pressed against my leg. I'm so comfy that the next thing I'm aware of is someone's light snoring. I blink my eyes open to see I'm lying on top of Rick in his bed, and when I glance to my side, Mich is lying right next to me on the bed too. I move myself slowly until I'm lying right in the middle of them both and freeze as Rick mutters something in his sleep. Then his arm wraps around my waist, and I can feel his heavy breathing near the top of my head. I rest my hand over Rick's arm, surprising myself with how comfy it is to be in the middle of them both. Mich's eyes slowly open as I look back at him, and he sees me staring.

"We can leave if you want," Mich whispers.

"No, don't," I say, and he nods, closing his eyes, and I do the same, happily falling straight back to sleep.

I stretch my arms out the next morning, surprised when I open my eyes and see Rick's bed is empty. I sit up, pushing the blanket off me and feeling that I'm still dressed in the clothes from last night which are now crumpled up. At least it is Thursday and no work today. I nearly jump out of my skin when Tay, in owl form, flies through the window, landing on the bed before turning back into her pixie self.

"You are still here...why?" she asks, and I scoot back on the bed.

"Because I'm their friend and live next door," I drawl. "I don't plan on going anywhere even if you want me to."

"Back to Frayan soon?" she asks, sounding hopeful.

"Nope. I was told not to go back to Frayan. Are you from there?" I ask her, and she nods.

"I am the last pixie of fate," she tells me, her voice small and quiet like she doesn't want to tell me that.

"Pixie of fate? Is that what your race is called?" I ask her.

"Yes. Your race made us to protect you, but you left, and we were killed over time for our magic," she says, and I feel so sorry for her. She is all alone. I wonder what she means by my race making hers. Maybe she means the Fray made her or something, as I doubt my shifter side did.

"Do you want to go back to Frayan?" I ask her, and she shakes her head.

"Earth is safer for me. I find family," she tells me, looking at the door. "Like you found family here too."

"I did," I whisper, and she actually smiles at me. I go to ask her why she wants me to go back to Frayan when the door opens and Rick walks in, naked with only a small blue towel wrapped around his waist. I cough on thin air as I gape at him, and he seems amused.

"I forgot to take clothes into the shower," he tells me and looks at Tay. "Is everything okay?"

"Yep," I answer, and Rick looks surprised for a second.

"Alright then. Anyway, Nath was making breakfast for you. You might want to go down before he goes to work and it gets cold," he tells me.

"Food?" Tay asks, and Rick only nods once before she quickly flies out of the room. That damn pixie is going to eat my food. I know it. Rick goes to his dresser, putting his back to me as he opens the drawer. I slide to sit on the end of the bed, looking at the tense muscles on his back, making myself be brave and blurt out the question I've wanted to ask for the last two weeks.

"Was I that bad of a kisser that you are avoiding

me now?" I ask, and he turns, holding some clothes as he gives me a confused look.

"That kiss was fucking amazing, don't say that again," he tells me and sighs at whatever he sees on my face. Rick walks over and sits next to me on the bed, putting his clothes to the side as I look up at him.

"Then why are you avoiding me?" I whisper the question.

"You are going out on a date with Nath...Mich looks at you like he wants more than a friend, and Josh...well I don't get Josh, but I wanted to give you space to decide what you want. I wasn't ignoring or avoiding you," he admits quietly, but I don't sense any lie in his words.

"It felt like you were," I confess.

"Adelaide, you are beautiful, smart and brave...I think you might be my mate," he blurts out to me, and I stare at him in shock.

"What?" I whisper.

"My wolf is very protective of you, and seeing you around the others isn't easy when we aren't mated. I didn't want to tell you what my wolf is thinking when all this is going on. I planned to see what happened when you are back at the castle and we could have more time together," he tells me, again all true.

"My wolf likes you too, but I don't know if we are mates," I tell him. I've heard that wolves can find their mates, but mum and dad never told me much about it.

"We need to shift together to find out, and I know you aren't ready for that. When you want to find out, I'm here," he tells me.

"And the date with Nath?" I lightly ask.

"Go. It will be fun, and I want the next date," he says. "I know there is some kind of bond between you two, and sharing lovers isn't something rare in the supernatural world. Hell, my stepmum has four mates."

"That must be hard work, four mates," I muse.

"It might be fun. Now, I need to get dressed and work out before going into work. You are more than welcome to stay and watch, but I think you might want to get downstairs before Tay eats all your pancakes," he says, and I quickly jump off the bed when he starts to undo his towel. I tell myself not to look back as I'm pulling the door shut behind me, but I can't help it when I do and see Rick naked from behind. Oh my god, he has a nice ass.

"Shut the door, Adelaide," Rick suggests, and I

giggle as I finish pulling the door shut. I walk to the stairs just as Nath runs up them, grinning when he sees me.

"Your cheeks are very red. They almost match your hair," he tells me. "Are you free Saturday?"

"Why?" I ask.

"Our date. I want to take you out at seven on Saturday. Unless you've changed your mind?" he asks me, looking a little worried.

"Erm, nope. A date sounds perfect," I reply, and he pulls me into a tight hug before putting me down.

"Food is on the table downstairs," he tells me, and I lean up, kissing his cheek.

"Thank you!" I say before sliding around him and running down the stairs. I walk into the kitchen, surprised to see my pancakes all in one piece and Tay eating off her own plate. Maybe Tay and I will get along after all.

CHAPTER
NINETEEN

I finish pulling my black leggings on and throwing my off-shoulder grey shirt on before glancing at myself in the mirror. It's one casual date. *Don't be nervous.* I brush my hair so it falls in nice waves over my right shoulder, stopping just over my ribs before walking out my bedroom. I leave my phone on the side, knowing I don't need it when I'm sure Nath has his. I walk down the stairs and slide my boots on before walking to the living room where Nath is waiting for me.

"You look perfect," he remarks, and I can't help but think the same of him. Nath's blond hair is trimmed a little, but somehow keeping that sexy messy feel to it. It makes you want to run your hands through his hair. He has a black leather jacket on, jeans and heavy looking boots that compliment his build.

"You said casual," I reply, feeling a little under-dressed for a date.

"Yeah, you can't wear a dress with what I have planned," he says with a smirk, standing up and handing me a leather jacket. "Put this on, you might get cold on the bike."

"Bike?" I ask, and he simply nods as I put the jacket on and zip it up. Nath slides his hand into mine and leads me out the house, where parked on the driveway behind my car is a dirt bike with giant wheels.

"Where the hell did you get that?" I ask, and Nath laughs.

"It's a hobby of mine. I have a garage in the village and a few of them around," he tells me. "I know most guys would take you out to a fancy meal or the cinema to watch a film, but those dates are forgettable. I don't want you to forget this."

"I have a feeling I won't," I mumble, and he tugs on my hand, leading me to the bike. Nath hands me a helmet before putting on his own and then helping me with the strap under my chin. He gets on the bike, and I sit behind him, wrapping my arms around his waist and pressing my head against his back.

"Ready?" Nath asks.

"Yes!" I reply and squeeze him tight as he speeds us across the street and into the woods right behind it. There is a dirt road already mapped out, and I laugh as he drives us at full speed all around the woods. We go up and down the hills and fly around bumpy corners until we get to a big field next to a lake. Nath parks the bike, and I get off first, pulling my helmet off.

"I brought us some food to eat," he explains, taking my helmet from me.

"A romantic picnic in the woods. I thought you didn't want to do the stereotypical dates," I tease him, and he laughs as he hooks our helmets on the bike handles and pulls the seat of the bike open, pulling out a bag.

"It's not that stereotypical," he replies, chuckling, and I walk to his side, sliding my hand into his as we walk over to the edge of the lake. We sit down on the grass together, just before the lake, so we can look across it. I'm happy it isn't raining today and it's peaceful here. Nath opens the bag and offers me the food he brought and a drink. I smile down at the ham, cheese and salad sandwiches he always makes me and how he knows I love blackcurrant fruit juice.

"Thank you," I mutter as he his own food out before pulling out a packet of Oreos, making my grin even bigger.

"I would never forget Oreos. Since you've been around, it's all we buy so that you and Rick have them," he says as he passes me the packet.

"Want to share?" I ask, opening the Oreo's.

"Love to," he replies with a small smile.

"I thought you could shift and have a run around if you want," Nath tells me, leaning back after finishing his food. "I know wolves get twitchy when they haven't shifted in a while."

"Yeah, just shifting in the house isn't good for my wolf. She gets testy," I laugh and lie back on the grass. I stare up at the sky, feeling Nath lie down next to me and watch the sky with me.

"Tell me something completely random about you," Nath asks me after a while. His fingers brush against my hand, and I move my hand closer, linking my fingers with his.

"I'm scared of the dark. Like the pitch black dark," I tell him, and he squeezes my hand.

"I'm sort of the opposite. I'm scared of the light of day, of people seeing me since I was brought up in the dark. I was hidden in it, and it is somewhat comforting that, even now, I can protect myself from the people in the daylight," he says, and I turn my head, staring at him as he looks at me. I have a feeling he hasn't taken his eyes off me for a while.

"Nath...you don't have to hide. None of us should ever have to hide because of what we are," I whisper, and he rolls onto his side, resting on his arm and leaning over me, our faces inches away.

"You're right, beautiful. Maybe there will be a world where we don't have to hide one day," he whispers. "Everything we are doing now is getting us closer to that goal."

"Do you wonder about Frayan? About going there because it's half of who we are?" I ask, because I can't stop thinking about the place the more I read in the books my mum left. They describe a world full of beauty and wonder, and it speaks to me in a way. It makes me want to desperately see the world I was born in. I know I can't ever go there, not after mum says someone is looking for me and it could mean death, but it doesn't stop me dreaming of it.

"Of course. The Fray are half my people, but it's not that easy. The Fray that came over in the war said portals only open twice a year for only a second if there is no one on the other side pulling them in," he explains to me.

"Pulling them in?" I ask.

"The Fray believe all people have connections that are hidden deep in their souls. That these connections are stronger than distance, than other worlds, than anything. Magic and souls are linked in Frayan, and it can be seen apparently," he whispers, and we both pause, staring at each other in silence for a second as tension builds between us. I go to kiss him at the same time he leans down to kiss me, and the first touch of our lips is like heat blasting all over my skin, and then it is quickly replaced by over-whelming pleasure. Nath must feel it too as he slides his hand to my waist, pulling me on top of him and never breaking the kiss in the movement.

"Adie," Nath groans against my lips as I rock against the hard bulge I can feel under his jeans. Nath's hands slide into my hair, kissing me deeper.

"Well...this is not what I expected to find two *cousins* doing..." Mr. Graves's highly sarcastic voice drawls, and I break away from Nath in shock, looking up to see Mr. Graves stood with at least twenty hunter guards, their guns pointed in our direction. I don't reply to him, looking down at Nath who utters one word.

"Run." Nath pushes me to the side and, in the blink of an eye, he is running straight towards the men, a blue shimmer spreading from his skin. I push myself to my feet, knowing I need to shift to help just as they start shooting at Nath with their guns. The dart bullets bounce off the shimmer surrounding Nath as he gets to the first two hunters, punching the one and sending him flying while the others run at him.

"Don't think about shifting or running. This will only hurt more if you do," Mr. Graves states and clicks his fingers. I scream as something slams into my neck as I go to run away, and pain shoots through my body. I fall to the floor, seeing Mr. Graves standing still as a statue as the wind moves his coat around. I focus on the sound of Nath roaring my name just as everything goes black.

CHAPTER
TWENTY

I gasp as I wake up, sitting up sharply and blinking my eyes at the bright white light in the room. I have to close my eyes and re-open them a few times to get used to how bright the room is. I remember everything in a rush and place my hand on my neck, feeling a metal collar strapped to my neck. It is quite thick, and I try to pull it away only to hear a quiet voice from the other side of the room.

"Don't pull it," the woman warns me, and I turn on the small bed to see a woman sat in the corner of the room, dressed in white trousers and a white shirt. She has red hair a similar colour to mine, but her roots have gone grey and her hair is cut very short. I glance around at the white painted walls,

180

the white tiles on the floor, and there is a massive glass mirror on the one wall. I don't know what this place is, but I bet it is in the hunter base. I swallow the ball of fear in my throat that Nath isn't here with me.

"Why?" I ask her. *Who is she and why am I with her?*

"It will burn your neck, and if you don't stop pulling, it would kill you," she tells me, her voice cracking a little, and as I look closer, I see her metal collar, with clear burn marks all around her neck.

"Who are you?" I ask her. I spot flower tattoos crawling up the side of her neck, but her shirt hides the design from me. They look red though, so perhaps roses.

"Asteria," she replies, turning her head to the side, and staring at me. "What is your name?"

"Adelaide," I reply, and her eyes widen, before she harshly starts shaking her head.

"No. No, you can't be. Adelaide is safe. Adelaide is not here. This is just a game!" the woman shouts, pressing herself against the wall, closing her eyes as she continues to shake her head muttering the word "no".

"I don't know who you think I am, but it doesn't matter. Are we in the hunter's base?" I ask her, but she ignores me, sinking to the floor to sit down and shaking her head continuously like she has lost her mind. I stare at the messy haired woman and wonder why they would put me in a room with her and why she cares what my name is. I walk to the door, feeling around the wall for any kind of handle or way to pull it, finding none. My wolf itches to get out when I step back and start to panic that I am trapped. When I put my hand to the collar, I know I can't shift. This thing would strangle me. I step back and pace around the room, walking past the woman who freezes and reaches out, grabbing my hand. I try to pull away, but she holds on tight as she uses her other hand to touch the crystals.

"You're really her. Only one of his children could wear this and live," she whispers, touching the crystals. "My Adelaide."

"Yours?" I ask her in surprise. *What the heck is she going on about?* I look down at her as she stares up at me with her bright green eyes that look awfully familiar. She goes to speak as the door opens, and I jump back as her hand falls away, watching as Mr. Graves walks in the room with two guards. The woman quickly stands up and places herself in front of me as one of the guards shuts the door.

"Protecting your daughter. How sweet," Mr.

Graves taunts, and I place my hand on Asteria's shoulder, walking to her side and looking at her.

"Daughter?" I ask, hearing my heart pound in my ears as I look over her features and finally to her eyes. My eyes. We have the same colour eyes, the same colour hair, and I know Graves isn't lying as I stare at her. She is my mother. The one who is meant to be dead. I don't know how to process any of it as I stare at her in pure shock. Only the sound of my heart beating, my heavy breathing and the feeling of my sweat collecting on my forehead is all I can process. I shake my head after a while, knowing he might be lying as the woman doesn't say anything. She could just be someone that looks like her.

"Oh, did your mother not tell you who she is?" Mr. Graves laughs. "Maybe I should be kind and fill you in on the past."

"My mum died, and my biological parents are dead. I don't want to hear your lies," I snap, sticking with denial.

"Adelaide," Asteria whispers, turning to face me and placing her hand on my cheek. "I am your mother. I left you with Reni, your mum, all those years ago and closed the last portal to Frayan. I thought it would kill me before the poison in my body did, but this monster found me. He locked me away here, testing on me and trying to use my powers for his own use." I stare in shock, the denial I was sticking to fading away because she couldn't know all of that unless she was telling me the truth.

"Until little Adelaide answered the door, I had almost given up on torturing Asteria to use her magic," Mr. Graves says, but I feel frozen in place as I stare at the woman claiming to be my mother.

"It can't be true," I croak out, shaking my head and feeling powerless as I start to realise she is telling me the truth.

"It is, and you know why I brought her to you, Asteria. Get on with it or I will kill her, slowly, in front of you until you do it," Graves demands.

"I can't. Adelaide is too young for that kind of power! I was over a hundred years old when I accepted my powers!" Asteria shouts, moving her hand away and protectively pushing me behind her. I just catch the subtle nod of Mr. Graves's head to the guard on his right before the guard steps forward. He slams my mother out of the way, and she screams as she hits the floor. I step back until my back hits the wall and the brown haired guard steps right in front of me. He leers as he grabs me by my hair and pushes me to my knees in front of him, turning my head to face my mother. She frantically looks around for something, anything to help me as I bite my lip from the pain of the guard pulling my hair. Graves straightens his suit before walking over to Asteria's side, picking out a remote from his pocket.

"Right, you have five chances. I will press this five times, and on the fifth time, she will die from the burns as her throat splits open. Don't make me keep pressing this, Asteria. Give her the power," he warns and holds the remote towards me, pressing a button. I scream as the collar burns my throat, the smell of my flesh burning is the only thing I can recognise outside of the incredible pain. I cough as the burn stops, and I shout in more pain as the guard lifts my head by my hair.

"Fine," Asteria gives in, tears pouring down her face as she crawls to me. The guard drops my hair and lets me go, stepping around us, but I keep my eyes on Asteria.

"The power of the royal Fray is passed from generation to generation. I hoped our family's power would die with me, and I am so sorry for the burden you receive now. This human wants you to use the gift for his benefit, but fate will decide who it is meant for," Asteria gently tells me, placing her hands on my shoulders.

"Get it over with!" Mr. Graves growls, making Asteria jump. She moves closer, grabbing my hands and placing them together before covering them with her own.

"When you get this gift, you will get all your powers. That includes the storm magic and your father's powers," she tells me, as our hands start to glow a deep red colour. "Make sure you kill them all, including me, then run." Our hands begin to glow red, then a blinding light blasts out. I scream as a burning feeling like electricity travels all up my arms, spreading across my body as the light gets brighter and brighter until the world goes black once more; this time I welcome it.

CHAPTER TWENTY-ONE

"**W**hat the fuck happened to you on your date, man?" Josh jokes as I walk through the door, but the minute he looks at the blood covering all my clothes, mixed in with the dirt, and the fury on my face, he quickly turns serious. "Where is Adelaide?"

"Taken by Graves. He had fuck knows how many hunters distract me while he took her. I thought he was there for both of us, but he only wanted her. I fucked up," I admit, remembering the sight of Graves's hunters picking up Adelaide's passed out form and taking her away as I fought the hunters trying to kill me.

"What did you just say?" Rick growls, storming

down the stairs, and Mich appears in the room, right in the middle of Josh and me.

"Adelaide is at the base and in trouble, we need to go. Now!" I demand, holding my hands in fists at my side.

"We can't raid the base alone. Not when he is expecting us to," Rick growls. "Fuck! I hate to say this, but Mich, go and get the kings and my step-mum." Mich nods and disappears, he doesn't need to be told more than once.

"Did they hurt her?" Rick demands, walking until he is right in front of me and placing his hands on my shoulders. "Are you hurt?"

"Yes, they hurt her, and I'm fine. One of those shock collars knocked her out," I tell him, remembering the heart-tearing scream that left her lips before she blacked out. I desperately tried to fight my way to her, but there were too many of them. By the time I killed the last of them, it was too late. They had taken her. I'm a fucking idiot.

"I'm going to get the weapons. Think of a plan," Josh tells us, and he walks straight up the stairs without looking back. The air next to us shimmers for a brief second before they appear. Queen Winter, King Atticus, King Dabriel, King Wyatt, King Jaxson and Mich all appear in a line together, looking downright terrifying even to me, and I've known them years.

"Rick, what has happened? Where is Josh?" Queen Winter demands, rushing to Rick and pulling his tall frame into a tight hug. Queen Winter looks about our age, but she is about ten years older and pregnant. I'm shocked the kings let her come here, but from what I remember, Queen Winter always did what she wanted.

"Josh is fine, just upstairs, and there is this girl —" Rick starts off and quickly gets cut off as Queen Winter's eyebrows shoot up as she looks up at Rick.

"What girl?" King Wyatt asks at the same time King Atticus asks. King Wyatt crosses his arms and glares at King Atticus, who only smirks. "Why have we not been told of *any* changes to this mission? This isn't a game, boy."

"With Winter..." Rick starts off, and Queen Winter steps back, crossing her arms over her little bump that you can see under her blue vest top.

"If you say because I'm pregnant—" she starts off and no doubt is going to tell him that her being pregnant isn't a reason for us all to risk our lives, but Rick cuts her off.

"Wait. Don't get mad. We don't have time for this," Rick growls, shaking his head. "She could be my mate. In fact, I'm nearly certain she is, and Graves has her. I can't let her die. I need your help...please."

"Mate?" King Jaxson mutters. "We need to have a long chat, Freds."

"Congrats, kid!" King Atticus says, holding a hand up for a high five, and everyone glares at him. "Not the time, alright I'll save it for later."

"Atti, go back to the castle and get the royal army ready in ten minutes," King Jaxson growls. "And bring me my sword."

"I'm coming with you as well," King Dabriel says, and Atti places his hand on King Dabriel's shoulder before they both disappear. Josh runs down the stairs, two bags of weapons in his hands, and he drops them on the floor.

"Get in here, man," King Atticus states, pulling Josh into a reluctant man hug just before Queen Winter gets to him, pulling Josh into an embrace as well. I look away when they start speaking quietly. I ignore them all, and grab one of the bags of weapons, picking it up and dropping it on the sofa in the lounge. I open it up and pull out my favourite swords, flipping them around in my hands. We are going to get her back, or I won't ever stop until she is safe. I know he wants her for something, so he won't kill her yet. If he kills her—

"What happened exactly?" King Wyatt asks, stopping my train of thought and stepping to my side. I don't answer him straight away as he starts going through the bag of weapons, pulling out the ones he doesn't want and dropping them on the other side of the sofa.

"I got distracted. They must have been waiting, and now she is gone," I explain.

"I didn't mean tonight. What exactly has been going on with this girl, and why have you all kept her a secret from us?" he asks.

"She just turned up and turned our lives upside down," I admit. "Thinking straight hasn't been a thing for us recently."

"Women tend to do that," King Wyatt lightly chuckles, his eyes drifting to Queen Winter before coming back to me as he picks a heavy sword up. "Does Rick know you're in love with his mate?"

"No," I admit.

"Secrets cause problems, and sharing does work if you can all be honest. You have all grown up together, don't lie and fall out because you won't talk about how you feel," King Wyatt tells me. "Make sure you tell your family the truth." I don't get a chance to reply to him as he walks away, and I look over to see Rick watching us closely. I'm well aware he could have heard our conversation from this distance, but he doesn't react in any way, so I doubt he did listen in. *Rescue Adie first and then deal with our feelings later.*

CHAPTER
TWENTY-TWO

I blink my eyes open, coughing on the dust that is somehow in my mouth and all around me, stinging my eyes. When the dust settles a little, I open my eyes to see a piece of wall in front of me, broken into pieces, and one of the larger pieces has an arm underneath it. I shake my head as I pull myself up, seeing the red flashing lights and hearing the blaring sound of an alarm in the distance. The room I'm in is destroyed, and I can't see anything but dust, rock, broken walls and glass. I glance down, seeing the broken collar by my hand and my other hand goes to my slightly burnt neck, pulling away when it stings as I touch it. I think back to my Asteria holding my hands, and then the pain and what I think was screams. *What happened?* I look back at the arm, hoping it's Asteria, and move to crawl across the floor to it. I pull the heavy bit of wall off the arm, and I'm relieved to see Asteria on the ground, covered in pieces of wall, but she is just waking up.

"Asteria?" I mutter her name, sliding an arm beneath her back and pulling her so she sits up.

"You remind me of your father," she says, her voice croaky. "Just as magical."

"You must have hit your head. We need to escape here, and you can tell me all about him. You can tell me everything, Asteria," I tell her, and she nods with a smile. I shakily stand myself up and hold a hand out for her. I manage to get her to stand up, but she nearly falls as she tries to put weight on her right leg, and I look down at all the blood pouring from it through her white trousers. "Put your arm around me." Asteria does as I ask, and we slowly make our way through the open door and into a long corridor. The flashing red light doesn't do much to show us where we need to go, but it does show me dozens of other doors down here.

"Call me mum. Just once," Asteria whispers to me.

"When we get out of here, I will. We need to find some stairs or something," I mutter, shifting Asteria's weight a little and deciding to head in the direction of the siren noise. We hobble down the corridor, and I glance to my right, seeing all the doors again and knowing I need to open these before we escape, or the guys' mission would be for nothing.

"What did you do to me in there?" I ask Asteria as we carry on walking slowly. "What happened?"

"You inherited your powers," she tells me.

"And then what caused the explosion or whatever happened to that room?" I ask. I seriously hope Graves and those hunters are dead under all the gravel and broken walls.

"You did. You are far more powerful than I was when I got my powers, but then with who your father is, that is no surprise," she muses, and I go to ask her who my father is when I see the flashing stairs sign. I hurry us towards it and pull the door open, stopping to stare at the emergency release button on the wall. I glance back down at the doors and wonder if it will open them. Only one way to find out. I lift the plastic covering and slam my hand onto the red button, and a blasting alarm sounds. The doors each start popping open one by one.

"We have to go," I remind myself and Asteria, knowing I've done my best to help them, and I need to get us out of here. The others can come back for the prisoners. I'm sure they are on their way to rescue us. I hope Nath has gotten out somehow, and I know I will go back for him if the others don't rescue him first. I help Asteria up the stairs, pausing every few steps with her to get our breaths back. I freeze when I hear steps below us, and three guys, carrying small children in their arms, run past us like we aren't even here. When I look down the staircase, there are more men, children and women slowly climbing the stairs behind us, all wearing those horrible white clothes. I have to pray Nath is with them. I slide my arm further around my mother's waist with more determination, and we carry on up the stairs, knowing we need to leave this place.

"Did you have a good childhood? Were you happy?" Asteria asks me, her voice breathless.

"Yes," I reply, trying not to break down emotionally right now. I can do that when I am somewhere safe and have some time to process this. Not right now.

"That's all I wanted. All we wanted for you. The throne is nothing without happiness," she says. "Everyone forgot that in Frayan."

"What throne?" I ask her as we keep walking.

"Yours. You are the heir to the Autumn court, Adelaide," she tells me as we get to the top of the stairs and make our way to the doorway right in front of us.

"That's crazy. I'm no princess, and you really must have hit your head," I tell her firmly.

"Being the heir to the throne is only half of who you are. The other half is far more powerful, and if you don't control it, embrace it, you will destroy everything like the prophecy said," she warns me, coughing on her words. I think back to the book and the mention of a prophecy in that book mum left me.

"Are you saying there is a prophecy about me?" I ask Asteria, and she nods.

"Yes, and I did everything to save you from it. I fear it has already started now," she says as we make our way across the reception room.

"What did you do?" I ask her, confused, and she goes to answer when three loud gunshots bang in the room and Asteria screams out in pain, falling out of my arm to the floor. I fall with her, not even looking for who shot her, as I turn her over onto her back.

"Adelaide. I never thought I'd get to see you one more time before death. This is a blessing, my sweet child...a blessing..." she whispers, her eyes fading, and then she starts to disappear. Her body slowly turns into red dust in my hands until there is nothing left but a pile of red dust that floats across the floor.

"Mum..." I crackle out, staring at the red dust in pure shock.

"She deserved to die. That bitch almost killed me. Now, Adelaide, be a smart girl and come here," Graves beckons, sounding not far behind me. Anger fills my mind, and my hands start to crackle with blue lightning.

"Adelaide, what are you doing?!" Mr. Graves's panicked voice shouts from behind me, but I see nothing but blue light as the lightning crackles all over my skin, and I stand up.

TWENTY-THREE

My body twitches in slight pain as I move us all to just inside the Hunter's Organisation base, and my hands fall to my knees once we appear as I bend over, getting my breath back. I've never moved this many people before.

"Impressive. I can only move forty, but you managed to move forty-two," King Atticus says, sounding as out of breath as I am. I glance at the competitive witch king and shake my head.

"This isn't a competition, guys," Queen Winter huffs, walking over to us. King Jaxson slides an arm around her waist, stopping her from going any further.

"You're staying right by my side, lass," he quietly tells her, but we all hear it. Josh rolls his eyes at the interaction and starts the walk towards the base, with Rick and Nath at his side.

"Let's go," I suggest, nodding my head at the base. We run silently towards the building, walking between the cars to get to the entrance. The royal army floods around the building, running in all directions to make sure we have all exits covered. We trained with the kings' royal army, and we know they move like one; they are as deadly as it gets. I pause next to Josh when he suddenly stops, and everyone does the same. I stare open-mouthed as all the hunters are running out of the building, not even glancing at us as they run. Mixed in between them are clearly prisoners, their white clothes are hard to miss. I gape in shock as Adelaide steps out of the building, every part of her body covered in blue energy, and blue lightning shoots out of the sky, hitting her body and making the blue energy grow larger. A hunter runs out the building, and she reaches a hand out, shooting blue lightning at him, turning him into dust in a second.

"Please say that's the girl," King Jaxson mutters, "because I don't fancy a fight against her, and I don't think we need to rescue her."

"Adie!" Rick shouts, stepping closer, but Adie doesn't even look his way as more blue lightning flashes across the sky, and she puts her hands up in the air. The lightning hits her hands, and she seems to just keep draining the lightning.

"We need to snap her out of it," I tell the others firmly.

"How do you suggest any of us do that?" King Dabriel asks, staring at Adelaide. "She looks very familiar."

"I don't care if she is familiar, we are moving back. Try to stop her or we will knock her out. You have a few minutes," King Jaxson states, pulling Queen Winter, King Wyatt, King Atticus and King Dabriel with him as they move back to the trees with the royal army not far behind.

"I can make a ward that covers me and get to her," I say, ignoring King Dabriel and thinking about it.

"She won't listen to you. You guys don't even get along," Rick snaps.

"And you don't know fucking everything, *prince* Fredrick. I'm the only one that can get close to her," I say, feeling like we need to do something before she takes in too much power. I think she is getting new powers and going through a change like we have at sixteen. This is what happens sometimes, and someone needs to stop her. People do change from the change, and I won't let Adie die for something like that.

"She could kill you," Rick warns. "That isn't Adie. Something has changed about her, and she is out of control."

"Then she kills me, or she kills us all. I have a feeling she is going to kill everyone near her soon," I say, knowing all that energy has to go somewhere.

"I have a better idea," Josh interrupts, "one that doesn't get any of us hurt."

"What?" I ask, shocked that Josh wants to help at all.

"Hold my coat, and stop me if I can't pull it back," Josh says, pulling his coat off and chucking it at me. I catch it and frown as I realise what he is going to do.

"Fucking hell, you're going to try and drain her with your demon powers?" Rick asks in shock. It's a terrible idea, but it might work.

"She seems like the type of girl I want to save and be the good guy for. So sure," Josh says, shocking us all and winking at Rick who goes to protest when Josh's eyes flash blue. I grab Rick's arm, making him step back when I know we can't stop Josh now. Josh is our best chance, and it's too late to stop the idiot anyway.

TWENTY-FOUR

"Sweetheart," Josh's soothing voice whispers to me, but I hold my hands in the air, seeing and feeling nothing but the lightning flashing through my body and blocking out the intense pain in my chest and the tears that I want to let fall. I can't fight my body, I can't fight the power controlling me, and I don't want to.

"You aren't here," I cry out.

"I am," he whispers, and I gasp as I feel like Josh is so close to me, but I'm too scared to open my eyes to look. I gasp again as I feel some of the power leaving me, feeling like it is drifting from my body.

"Why would you come for me? You don't even like me," I ask, knowing this is just my imagination.

"I want to save you," Josh tells me.

"Why?" I cry out, the words feeling painful to say. "I'm not worth saving."

"Because you *are* worth saving, Adelaide. You are worth fighting to save, and I am here for you," he tells me, his words feeling soothing.

"I'm scared to let go of the power. I'm scared to open my eyes and you won't really be there," I whisper, my voice cracking. "My parents are dead, my mother is dead, and everything is so wrong. I am alone."

"No. You have a pack. You have us and Sophie. We need you, now let go. I will catch you," Josh whispers, his voice is so seductive that I open my eyes. Blue energy bounces everywhere, making it hard to see, and the lightning is crackling around all of my skin. Josh doesn't let that scare him as he stalks through the storm like there is nothing there. Like there is nothing that would stop him from getting to me. My power doesn't touch him, letting him walk to me with his glowing blue eyes. Josh holds a hand out to me.

"I thought you didn't like me, yet you're really here," I gasp, seeing his blue eyes, and the blue veins crawling from his eyes. He is using his demon powers.

"Take my hand and let the power go," Josh demands. "I like you, Adie, and I'm here."

I stare up at the lightning flashing from the skies before meeting Josh's eyes again, and I lower my hands slowly, staring at the crackling electric sparks covering them before moving my hand and sliding it into Josh's. The moment our hands touch, a massive boom sends everything around us flying away in a whirlwind of blue energy, and we are left holding hands, staring at each other as Josh's eyes fade back to their normal blue. I'm smiling when suddenly, my knees give out, but Josh sweeps me into his arms before I can fall.

"Thank you," I whisper, wrapping my arms around his neck.

Josh wordlessly carries me over to the others, gently putting me on my feet, and Rick wraps his arms around me first in a tight embrace.

"Are you okay?" he asks, and I nod, still feeling dizzy as I try to stand on my own. Nath's eyes meet mine over Rick's shoulder, and he smiles at me, looking relieved, but there is guilt in his eyes that I don't understand. I look up in shock as an owl flies out of the trees, landing on my shoulder, and I stare into its pink eyes, recognising the owl as Tay. *Was she worried about me?*

"Maybe I should have a look at her?" a male voice says behind us, and I turn to see an angel walking over to us, a woman holding his hand. The man is a light angel I suspect, with his white hair, purple eyes and white wings. The woman is a little shorter than me, with long dark brown hair and a kind smile as she holds her hand out to me.

"I'm Winter, nice to meet you," the woman says. I step away from Rick and to Josh's side as I reach for her hand as I introduce myself.

"I'm Adelaide," I say, sliding my hand into hers. Her eyes widen in shock, and she falls to the floor, holding her hand as she screams in pain. The angel looks at me in horror, falling to the woman's side, wrapping an arm around her shoulders. Dozens of people start running out from the trees towards us, and I step closer to Josh, feeling confused. *Did I hurt her?*

"Run!" Winter screams just as a blurry blue wave of light appears in front of us. I go to run when the light seems to pull me into it, and I can do nothing but let it. The last thing I see is Josh grabbing my hand before the light burns so bright that everything real is lost as we start falling, and a voice whispers to me:

· · ·

*THE TRUE PROPHESIED queen of the Fray comes home...
with death as her shadow.*

EPILOGUE

I rub my wrist, tears streaming down my face as I stare into the heartbroken eyes of Freddy who stares at the spot where Adelaide, the strange owl, and Josh just were. They are gone. The promise is paid.

"What did you do, Winter?" Freddy demands in shock. "What the hell did you do? Where are they?"

Dabriel helps me stand up, holding me close as the others get to us.

"I made a promise in the war to a Fray queen. I was told I would meet a half Fray...a royal of their kind, and that I would send her back," I tell them all honestly. "I was tricked, and Queen Lilyanne is a monster."

"How could you do that to a person you don't

even know?" Freddy asks in disgust, and it breaks my heart to see him looking at me like this. Mich and Nath haven't even moved, they look confused and destroyed. They all love her...and this is my fault.

"It wasn't her choice. The war *had* to be won, and Winter couldn't have known she would be your mate, Freddy," Jax says, stepping to my side just as the others get closer. "Are you okay? The baby okay?"

"I'm fine," I whisper.

"We have to go to Frayan. Now," Mich demands, placing his hand on Freddy's shoulder. "We have to save Adie and Josh."

"I know a way. Over the years, I researched a way to rescue the girl I had to send. I never planned to just send anyone to the monster I made the promise to," I say, thinking back to the Fray in my castle. There is one way to get there, but it is a one-way trip.

"Then send us there," Nath demands. "We have to find them both."

"We will find her and save her," Freddy firmly replies, sounding like his uncle and father. Sounding like a king.

"I didn't know," I whisper, still in shock.

"It doesn't matter now. Adelaide needs us," Freddy says, but he won't look at me.

"The key is at the castle," I say, staring at them all. I just hope they can forgive me if anything happens to her. I know I couldn't forgive myself.

"It's not your fault," Jax whispers, sliding an arm around my waist as I stare at Nath, Mich and Freddy as they talk between themselves.

"If she dies, it will be my fault."

Keep reading with Adelaide's Trust...

ABOUT G. BAILEY

G. Bailey is a USA Today and international bestselling author of books that are filled with everything from dragons to pirates. Plus, fantasy worlds and breath-taking adventures.
G. Bailey is from the very rainy U.K. where she lives with her husband, two children, three cheeky dogs and one cat who rules them all.

(You can find exclusive teasers, random giveaways and sneak peeks of new books on the way in Bailey's Pack on Facebook or on TIKTOK— gbaileybooks)

FIND MORE BOOKS BY G. BAILEY ON AMAZON...

LINK HERE.

PART ONE
BONUS READ OF
HER WOLVES

DESCRIPTION

**I knew nothing about mates until the alpha
rejected me...**

Growing up in one of the biggest packs in the world,
I have my life planned out for me from the second I
turn eighteen and find my true mate in the moon
ceremony.
Finding your true mate gives you the power to share
the shifter energy they have, given to the males of
the pack by the moon goddess herself. The power to
shift into a wolf.
But for the first time in the history of our pack, the
new alpha is mated with a nobody. A foster kid
living in the pack's orphanage with no ancestors or
power to claim.

Me.

After being brutally rejected by my alpha mate, publicly humiliated and thrown away into the sea, the dark wolves of the Fall Mountain Pack find me. They save me. The four alphas. The ones the world fears because of the darkness they live in.

In their world? Being rejected is the only way to join their pack. The only way their lost and forbidden god gives them the power to shift without a mate.

I spent my life worshipping the moon goddess, when it turns out my life always belonged to another...

This is a full-length reverse harem romance novel full of sexy alpha males, steamy scenes, a strong heroine and a lot of sarcasm. Intended for 17+ readers. This is a trilogy.

CHAPTER
ONE

⟩ ⟩ ● ⟨ ⟨

"Don't hide from us, little pup. Don't you want to play with the wolves?"

Beta Valeriu's voice rings out around me as I duck under the staircase of the empty house, dodging a few cobwebs that get trapped in my long blonde hair. Breathlessly, I sink to the floor and wrap my arms around my legs, trying not to breathe in the thick scent of damp and dust. Closing my eyes, I pray to the moon goddess that they will get bored with chasing me, but I know better. No goddess is going to save my ass tonight. Not when I'm being hunted by literal wolves.

I made a mistake. A big mistake. I went to a party in the pack, like all my other classmates at the beta's house, to celebrate the end of our schooling and, personally for me, turning eighteen. For some tiny reason, I thought I could be normal for one night. Be like them.

And not just one of the foster kids the pack keeps alive because of the laws put in place by a goddess no one has seen in hundreds of years. I should have known the betas in training would get drunk and decide chasing me for another one of their "fun" beatings would be a good way to prove themselves.

Wiping the blood from my bottom lip where one of them caught me in the forest with his fist, I stare at my blood-tipped fingers in a beam of moonlight shining through the broken panelled wall behind me.

I don't know why I think anyone is going to save me. I'm nothing to them, the pack, or to the moon goddess I pray to every night like everyone in this pack does.

The moon goddess hasn't saved me from shit.

Heavy footsteps echo closer, changing from crunching leaves to hitting concrete floor, and I know they are in the house now. A rat runs past my leg, and I nearly scream as I jolt backwards into a loose metal panel that vibrates, the metal smacking against another piece and revealing my location to the wolves hunting me.

Crap.

My hands shake as I climb to my feet and slowly step out into the middle of the room as Beta Valeriu comes in with his two sidekicks, who stumble to his side. I glance around the room, seeing the staircase is broken and there is an enormous gap on the second floor. It looks burnt out from a fire, but there is no other exit. I'm well and truly in trouble now. They stop in an intimidating line, all three of them muscular and jacked up enough to knock a car over. Their black hair is all the same shade, likely because they are all cousins, I'm sure, and they have deeply tanned skin that doesn't match how pale my skin is. Considering I'm a foster kid, I could have at least gotten the same looks as them, but oh no, the moon goddess gave me bright blonde hair that never stops growing fast and freckly pale skin to stand out. I look like the moon comparing itself to the beauty of the sun with everyone in my pack.

Beta Valeriu takes a long sip of his drink, his eyes flashing green, his wolf making it clear he likes the hunt. Valeriu is the newest beta, taking over from his father, who recently retired at two hundred years of age and gave the role to his son willingly. But Valeriu is a dick. Simple as. He might be good-looking, like most of the five betas are, but each one of them lacks a certain amount of brain cells. The thing is, wolves don't need to be smart to be betas, they just need the right bloodline and to kill when the alpha clicks his fingers.

All wolves like to hunt and kill. And damn, I'm always the hunted in this pack.

"You know better than to run from us, little Mairin. Little Mary the lamb who runs from the wolf," he sing songs the last part, taking a slow step forward, his shoe grating across the dirt under his feet. Always the height jokes with this tool. He might be over six foot, and sure, my five foot three height isn't intimidating, but has no one heard the phrase *small but deadly*?

Even if I'm not even a little deadly. "Who invited you to my party?"

"The entire class in our pack was invited," I bite out.

He laughs, the crisp sound echoing around me like a wave of frost. "We both know you might be in this pack, but that's only because of the law about killing female children. Otherwise, our alpha would have ripped you apart a long time ago."

Yeah, I know the law. The law that states female children cannot be killed because of the lack of female wolves born into the pack. There is roughly one female to five wolves in the pack, and it's been that way for a long time for who knows what reason. So, when they found me in the forest at twelve, with no memories and nearly dead, they had to take me in and save my life.

A life, they have reminded me daily, has only been given to me because of that law. The law doesn't stop the alpha from treating me like crap under his shoe or beating me close to death for shits and giggles. Only me, though. The other foster kid I live with is male, so he doesn't get the "special" attention I do. Thankfully.

"We both know you can't kill me or beat me bad enough to attract attention without the alpha here. So why don't you just walk away and find some poor dumbass girl to keep you busy at the party?" I blurt out, tired of all this. Tired of never saying what I want to these idiots and fearing the alpha all the time. A bitter laugh escapes Valeriu's mouth as his eyes fully glow this time. So do his friends', as I realise I just crossed a line with my smart-ass mouth.

My foster carer always said my mouth would get me into trouble.

Seems he is right once again.

A threatening growl explodes from Beta

Valeriu's chest, making all the hairs on my arms stand up as I take a step back just as he shifts. I've seen it a million times, but it's always amazing and terrifying at the same time. Shifter energy, pure dark forest green magic, explodes around his body as he changes shape. The only sound in the room is his clicking bones and my heavy, panicked breathing as I search for a way out of here once again, even though I know it's pointless.

I've just wound up a wolf. A beta wolf, one of the most powerful in our pack.

Great job, Irin. Way to stay alive.

The shifter magic disappears, leaving a big white wolf in the space where Valeriu was. The wolf towers over me, like most of them do, and its head is huge enough to eat me with one bite. Just as he steps forward to jump, and I brace myself for something painful, a shadow of a man jumps down from the broken slats above me, landing with a thump. Dressed in a white cloak over jeans and a shirt, my foster carer completely blocks me from Valeriu's view, and I sigh in relief.

"I suggest you leave before I teach you what an experienced, albeit retired, beta wolf can do to a young pup like yourself. Trust me, it will hurt, and our alpha will look the other way."

The threat hangs in the air, spoken with an authority that Valeriu could never dream of having in his voice at eighteen years old. The room goes silent, filled with thick tension for a long time before I hear the wolf running off, followed by two pairs of footsteps moving quickly. My badass foster carer slowly turns around, lowering his hood and brushing his long grey hair back from his face. Smothered in wrinkles, Mike is ancient, and to this day, I have no clue why he offered to work with the foster kids of the pack. His blue eyes remind me of the pale sea I saw once when I was twelve. He always dresses like a Jedi from the human movies, in long cloaks and swords clipped to his hips that look like lightsabres as they glow with magic, and he tells me this is his personal style.

His name is even more human than most of the pack names that get regularly overused. My name, which is the only thing I know about my past thanks to a note in my hand, is as uncommon as it gets. According to an old book on names, it means Their Rebellion, which makes no sense. Mike is apparently a normal human name, and from the little interaction I've had with humans through their technology, his name couldn't be more common.

"You are extremely lucky my back was playing

up and I went for a walk, Irin," he sternly comments, and I sigh.

"I'm sorry," I reply, knowing there isn't much else I can say at this point. "The mating ceremony is tomorrow, and I wanted one night of being normal. I shouldn't have snuck out of the foster house."

"No, you should not have when your freedom is so close," he counters and reaches up, gently pinching my chin with his fingers and turning my head to the side. "Your lip is cut, and there is considerable bruising to your cheek. Do you like being beaten by those pups?"

"No, of course not," I say, tugging my face away, still tasting my blood in my mouth. "I wanted to be normal! Why is that so much to ask?"

"Normal is for humans and not shifters. It is why they gave us the United Kingdom and Ireland and then made walls around the islands to stop us from getting out. They want normal, and we need nothing more than what is here: our pack," he begins, telling me what I already know. They agreed three hundred years ago we would take this part of earth as our own, and the humans had the rest. No one wanted interbreeding, and this was the best way to keep peace. So the United Kingdom's lands were separated into four packs. One in England, one in Wales, one in Scotland and one in Ireland. Now there are just two packs, thanks to the shifter wars: the Ravensword Pack that is my home, who worship the moon goddess, and then the Fall Mountain Pack, who owns Ireland, a pack we are always at war with. Whoever they worship, it isn't our goddess, and everything I know about them suggests they are brutal. Unfeeling. Cruel.

Which is exactly why I've never tried to leave my pack to go there. It might be shit here, but at least it's kind of safe and I have a future. Of sorts.

"Do you think it will be better for me when I find my mate tomorrow?" I question...not that I want a mate who will control me with his shifter energy. But it means I will shift into a wolf, like every female can when they are mated, and I've always wanted that.

Plus, a tiny part of me wants to know who the moon goddess herself has chosen for me. The other half of my soul. My true mate. Someone who won't see me as the foster kid who has no family, and will just want me.

Mike looks down at me, and something unreadable crosses his eyes. He turns away and starts walking out of the abandoned house, and I jog to catch up with him. Snowflakes drop into my blonde hair as we head through the forest, back to the foster home, the place I will finally leave one way or another tomorrow. I pull my leather jacket around my chest, over my brown T-shirt for warmth. My torn and worn out jeans are soaked with snow after a few minutes of walking, the snow becoming thicker with every minute. Mike is silent as we walk past the rocks that mark the small pathway until we get to the top of the hill that overlooks the main pack city of Ravensword.

Towering buildings line the River Thames that flows through the middle of the city. The bright lights make it look like a reflection of the stars in the sky, and the sight is beautiful. It might be a messed up place, but I can't help but admire it. I remember the first time I saw the city from here, a few days after I was found and healed. I remember thinking I had woken up from hell to see heaven, but soon I learnt heaven was too nice of a word for this place. The night is silent up here, missing the usual noise of the people in the city, and I silently stare down wondering why we have stopped.

"What do you see when you look at the city, Irin?"

I blow out a long breath. "Somewhere I need to escape."

I don't see his disappointment, but I easily feel it.

"I see my home, a place with darkness in its corners but so much light. I see a place even a foster wolf with no family or ancestors to call on can find happiness tomorrow," he responds. "Stop looking at the stars for your escape, Irin, because tomorrow you will find your home in the city you are trying so hard to see nothing but darkness in."

He carries on walking, and I follow behind him, trying to do what he has asked, but within seconds my eyes drift up to the stars once again.

Because Mike is right, I am always looking for my way to escape, and I always will. I wasn't born in this pack, and I came from outside the walls that have been up for hundreds of years. That's the only explanation for how they found me in a forest with nothing more than a small glass bottle in my hand and a note with my name on it. No one knows how that is possible, least of all me, but somehow I'm going to figure it out. I have to.

CHAPTER
TWO

)) ● ((

"**W**ake up. You have a book on your face."

Blinking my eyes open, I see nothing but blurry lines until I lift the book I was reading off my face and rub my nose. Damn, I must have fallen asleep reading again. I close the human-written romance book about demons at an academy and turn my gaze to where my foster brother is holding the door open. Jesper Perdita has dark brown, overgrown hair that falls around his face and shoulders, and his clothes are all a little too big for him and torn in places because they are hand-me-downs. But he smiles every single damn day, and for that alone, I love him. At just eight, he acts the same age as me thanks to losing his family a year ago and having no relatives offer to take him in. I don't care that we aren't blood-related, somehow I'm always going to be here for him, because he hasn't had a childhood any more than I have. We are foster kids in a pack that hates our very existence, and they make damn sure we know about it.

The fact they keep him alive is just because one day he might have a powerful wolf when he turns sixteen. If he doesn't, he won't have any family to save him from what happens next. I'm a little luckier in the sense I will find a mate, every female always does at the mating ceremony in the year they turn eighteen, and my mate will have no choice but to keep me alive. Even if he hates who I am, our fate is linked from the second the bond is shown.

"What time is it, Scrubs?" I ask, needing to pull my thoughts from the ceremony to anything else before I freak out. He twitches his nose at my nick-name. That came from how many times he needed to scrub his face of dirt and mud every single day. He is the messiest kid I've ever seen, and it's awesome. I want a different future for him, one where he could have the same last name as everyone in the pack other than the foster kids. We are given the last name Perdita, which means *lost* in Latin, because we are lost in every sense of the word.

Everyone else in the pack shares the same last name as the pack alpha. Ravensword.

"Six in the morning. We have to leave for the ceremony in an hour, and Mike said you need to bathe and wear the dress in the bathroom," he answers. He looks down, nervously kicking his foot. "Mike said something about brushing your hair so it doesn't look like a bat's nest."

I snort and run my hand through my blonde hair. Sure...I might not have brushed it a lot, but the unruly waves don't want to be tamed.

"I won't go, get a mate and never come back. You know that, right?" I ask him, sliding myself out of my warm bed and into the much colder room. Snowflakes line my bedroom window that is slightly cracked open, and I walk over, pushing it shut before looking back at Jesper. He meets my gaze with his bright blue eyes, but he says nothing.

"Whoever finds out you're their mate is going to want you to start fresh. Without this place and me following you around. I might be eight, but I'm not stupid," he replies. Floorboards creak under my feet as I walk over to him and pull him in for a hug, resting my head on top of his. The truth is, I can't promise him much. The males in mating have control over the females, and to resist that control is painful, so I'm told. That's why the moon goddess is the only one who can choose a mate for us, because if it went wrong, it would be a disaster for all involved.

"If my mate does, then I will figure out a way to get him to let me see you. The moon goddess will not give me a mate I am going to hate. All mates love each other," I tell him what I've heard.

"I don't like goodbyes," he replies, pulling away from me. "So I won't come with you today. I won't."

"I get it, kid," I say as he walks to the stairs. He never looks back, and I'm proud of him, even if it hurts to watch him make another choice that only adults should have to make. I head back into my small bedroom, which has a single bed with white sheets and a squeaky mattress, and one chest of drawers. I grab my towels and head down the stairs to the only bathroom in the old, very quirky house. The bathroom is through the first door in the corridor, and I shut the door behind me, not bothering to switch the light on as it is bright enough in here from the light pouring through the thin windows at the top of the room. Peeling dolphin-covered wallpaper lines every wall, and the porcelain clawfoot bathtub is right in the middle of the room. A cream toilet and a row of worn white cabinets line the other side, with a sink in the middle of them. Hanging on the back of the door is the dress I have dreaded to see and yet wanted to because it's the nicest thing I am likely ever going to wear.

The mating dress is a custom-made dress for every woman in the pack, paid for by the alpha to celebrate the joy-filled day, and each is made to worship the moon goddess herself. Mine is no different. My dress is pure silk and softer than I could have imagined as I run my fingers over it. The hem of the dress is lined with sparkling white crystals, and the top part of the dress is tight around the chest and stomach. The bottom half falls like a ball-gown, heavier than the top and filled with dozens of silk layers that shimmer as I move them.

As I stare at the dress, the urge to run away fills me. The urge to run to the sea and swim to the wall to see if there is any way to get out. Any way to escape the choices I have been given in life.

Mike was right, I can't see the light in the pack, because the darkness smothers too much. It takes too much.

I step away until the back of my legs hit the cold bathtub, and I sink down to the floor, wrapping my arms around my legs and resting my head on top of my knees.

One way or another, the mating ceremony is going to change everything for me.

"Do hurry, Irin. We have a four-hour drive, and this is not a day you should be late like every other day of your life!" Mike shouts through the door, banging on it twice.

"On it!" I shout back, crawling to my feet and pushing all thoughts of trying to escape to the back of my mind. It was a stupid idea, anyway. The pack lands are heavily guarded, and they would scent me a mile off. After a quick bath to wipe the dirt off me and wash my hair, I brush my wavy hair until it falls to my waist in bouncy locks, even when I know the wind will whip them up into a storm as soon as I'm outside. The dress is easy to slip on, and I wipe the mirror of the steam to look at myself after pulling my boots on.

My green eyes, the colour of moss mixed with specks of silver, look brighter this morning against my pale skin, framed by blonde, almost golden, hair. I look as terrified as I feel about today, but this is what the moon goddess wants, and she is our ancestor. The first wolf to howl at the moon and receive the power to shift.

She will not let me down today.

I nod at myself, like a total loser, and walk out of

the bathroom to find Mike and my other foster brother waiting for me. Mike huffs and walks away, mumbling something about a lamb to the slaughter under his breath, and I look at Daniel instead. His brown eyes are wide as he looks at me from head to toe, likely realising for the first time the best friend he has is actually a girl. He is used to me in jeans or baggy clothes, following him through the muddy forest and not giving a crap if every single one of my nails is broken by the end.

And I never wear dresses. Not like this. Daniel runs his hand through his muddy-brown hair that needs a cut before he smiles.

"Shit, you look different, Irin," he comments with a thick voice. Daniel is one year older than me, and when he was tested for his power last year, he was found to be an extremely powerful wolf. He is next in line to be a beta if anyone dies, which would be a big thing for a foster kid to be a beta. Either way, he is free of this place, and who knows, he might even be my mate. A small part of me hopes so because Daniel is my best friend, and it would be so easy to spend my life with him. I don't know about romance, as I have never seen him like that. He is good-looking in a rugged way, so I guess we could figure it out.

"Nervous about today?" I ask him, as this is his second mating ceremony, and it's likely he might find a mate. It's usually the second or third ceremony where males find their mates, but for females, it's always the first.

He clears his throat and meets my eyes. "Yeah, but who wouldn't be?"

"Me. I'm totally cool with it," I sarcastically reply. He laughs and walks over, pulling me into a tight hug like he always does. This time, I hear his wolf rumble in his chest, the vibrations shaking down my arms.

"If you're mated to a tool, I'll help you kill him and hide the body. Got it?" he tells me, and I laugh at his joke until he leans back, placing his hands on my shoulder. He moves one of his hands and tips my chin up so I'm looking at him. "I'm not joking, Irin. I don't care who it is, they aren't fucking around with you."

"Mates are always a perfect match," I reply, twitching my nose. "Why would you think—"

He lowers his voice as he cuts me off. "You don't live in the city like I do, and I can tell you now, mates are not a perfect match. Not even close. The moon goddess...well, I don't know what she is doing, but you need to be cautious. Very cautious because of your background."

"Why didn't you tell me this before?" I demand.

He shrugs. "Guess I didn't want you to overthink it and try to run. I can't save you from what they'd do if you ran, but I can protect you from a shitty mate. I.e., threaten to break every bone in his body if he hurts you."

"Daniel—" I'm cut off as Mike comes back into the corridor and clears his throat.

"Get in the car, now. It looks bad on me when we are late!" he huffs, holding the front door open. Daniel uses his charming smile to make Mike's lips twitch in laughter as I hurry to the front door and step out into the freezing cold snow. It sinks into my dress and shoes, but I welcome the icy stillness to the air, forcing me to stop over worrying for a second.

"Always daydreaming, this one," Mike mutters as he passes me, talking to Daniel at his side. "Her eyes are going to get stuck looking up in the clouds one day."

"At least I'd be seeing a pretty view for the rest of my life," I call after Mike as I hurry after them down the path to the old car waiting by the road. We don't use cars often, only today and travelling to funerals is permitted, mostly because the cars are old junk that make a lot of noise and take up fuel. Daniel pulls the yellow rusty door to the car open, and I slide inside to the opposite seat before doing up my seatbelt as Daniel and Mike get in the car. Mike drives and Daniel sits next to me rather than shotgun.

About ten minutes into the drive, I realise why Daniel sits next to me as my hands shake and he covers my hand with his.

Please, moon goddess, choose Daniel or someone decent. I don't want to become a mate murderer in my first year as a wolf.

THREE

)) ● ((

Flickering, multicoloured lights drift across my eyes as I wake up, finding my head lying on Daniel's broad shoulder, his arm wrapped around my waist, and it's so unexpected, I jolt up, almost hitting my head against Daniel's chin. He moves super fast, with reflexes his wolf gives him, and just misses my head. I slide out of Daniel's arm, and he clears his throat, straightening up on his seat and running a hand through his thick hair. Rather than talk about that awkward moment, I turn and look out the window, frost stuck to its edges, to see we are driving down by a cliff that overlooks the glittering sea between Wales and Ireland. I've been to this place once when I was fifteen on a school trip to see where a mating ceremony is held and what we should expect for our future.

If anywhere in this world made me believe in magic, it was this place. A place that has been in my dreams for so many years. For most wolves, this is the place they will meet their wolves and start their new life. For me, it's a way of escaping my past and finally finding out what the moon goddess wants for me. It can't be this life I have, the torture at the hands of pack leaders, the pain of being an outcast with no family.

I catch Mike's eyes in the middle mirror and see a little sadness in them like always, because he has heard and seen all the horrors the pack has forced on me throughout the years. Protecting me was something he has struggled to do, because, at the end of the day, he couldn't be everywhere.

"Nearly here, aren't we?" Daniel interrupts my thoughts, and I'm thankful for it. That's a dark memory lane to go down. "They should let you wear a coat over the dress, it's freezing."

"I've never cared about the cold," I remind him, gazing back out of the window as we pull up in the gravelled area by the cliff. Several groups of people are standing around or walking down the stone cliff pathway to the beach that is marked with fire lanterns on wooden poles every few metres, making the walk look eerie and frightening.

"You can do this, Irin. You've been brave ever since you were found in the woods, half-starved, dirty and alone. Look at you now," Mike tells me as he turns the car off, meeting my line of sight through the mirror. "You are a woman this pack will be honoured to have. Now hold your head high, put the past away and show them. Show them who you are, Irin."

My cheeks feel red and hot as I wipe a few tears away and force my hands to stop shaking as I grab the handle of the door. I can't tell him, not without my voice catching, that I will miss Mike and his words of wisdom. His kindness and general attitude towards life, the ways he has shown me how to be strong even at my lowest points. Pulling the door handle open, I step out onto the lightly snow-covered ground, and the cold, brittle sea air slams into me, making me shiver from head to toe. I can taste the salt in the air and smell the water of the sea and hear it crashing against the sand below us. The wind whips my hair around my face as Daniel walks past me, looking back once before he walks down the path to join the other men at the beach where they have to stand. Mike moves to my side, and we simply wait as all the men leave for the path down to the beach, while the women, us, wait at the top for our time to descend.

Some parents linger for a while before they walk to the edge of the cliff in the distance where there's a massive crowd of spectators waiting to watch the magic of the mating ceremony. Mike leaves eventually to join them, never glancing back at me. The girls all gather, pretending I don't exist like they always have done since I turned up at their school. A small, tiny part of me hurts that not a single one of the forty-two girls in my class who have known me six years even looks my way.

I'm invisible to them, to my pack, to everyone.

Rubbing my chest, I gulp when the bell rings. A single, beautiful bell ring fills the air to start the beginning of the mating ceremony, and tension rings through the air as everyone goes silent. Like ducks in a row, the women all line up, and of course I move right to the back, behind Lacey Ravensword, someone who has never even looked my way, even though she is considered a low potential mate because of her father trying to run away from the pack, and he was killed when she was a toddler. Even she, with her family basically betrayers to the alpha himself, is higher ranked than I am. She flicks her dark brown hair over her shoulder, glancing back at me and sneering once with her beautiful face before turning away.

The cold seeps into my bones by the time the line moves enough for me to walk, and my legs feel stiff with every step, the nerves making me feel so close to passing out right here and now. Every single step off the cliff and down the path feels torturous until I see the beach.

Then everything fades into nothing but pure magic. In the centre of the sandy yellow beach is a massive archway, sculpted into two wolves with their noses touching where they meet in the middle. The wolves are so high the tips of their ears touch the heavy clouds above us, and icicles line the grooves of the fur on their snow-tipped backs. In the centre of the archway, one of the first females steps into the pool of water under the archway, sinking all the way under completely before rising and swimming slowly through the archway. The water suddenly glows green, lit up with magic from the moon goddess herself.

The young lady with long black hair climbs out of the pool on the other side, her entire body glowing green with magic, and the magic slowly slips from her skin, turning itself into a swirling ball of energy and shooting away from her. It flies into the crowd of wolf shifter men waiting on the other side, all of them too hard to really see from here, and there are cheers when the mate or mates are no doubt found. I can't see who the female goes to as the cliff winds around, but I hope she is happy with her new mates. Daniel's warnings about mates not always being happy fills my mind, making me more nervous than ever before, because what if he is right? What if I end up with a mate who I hate and he hates me?

I trip on a small rock, slamming down onto the path and hissing as my hand is cut. I look up as Lacey turns back, and then she just laughs, leaving me on my knees on the path as she carries on behind the queue. Tears fill my eyes that I refuse to let fall, and I stand up, seeing my dress is now dirty with sand and mud, and I lift my hand to see blood dripping down my palm to my wrist from a long cut. Sighing, I close my palm and let my blood drop against the wet sand as I know I have to carry on down this path.

What feels like forever later, I get to the beach and look across to see Lacey waiting behind three other classmates, just as one of them steps into the water. Four left before my fate is decided. I'm tempted to slip my shoes off, to enjoy the feel of the cold sand under my bare feet, but I keep my boots on. I don't want to lose them. I walk over the beach, feeling so many eyes watching and judging me. I refuse to look at the men on the other side, knowing the new alpha will be there, and seeing him brings up so many dark memories. He was just the alpha's son back then, back when we were fifteen and he tricked me by pretending to be my friend.

Now he is the alpha, at only eighteen, after he ripped his father to pieces four months ago. The pack is scared of him, but me?

He terrifies me.

Keeping my eyes down, I only look up to see Lacey step into the water with perfect poise and elegance I could never master in my wildest dreams. She sinks under the water, and it glows bright green, and this close, I can feel the magic like it's pulling me towards it. The water is enchanting, and I can't take my eyes off it until the glow fades, and I glance up to see the magic surrounding Lacey as she stands on the other side of the pool. The magic leaves her body and gathers in a ball, before slamming left and straight into the chest of one of the men near the front.

Not just any man.

Daniel.

He stands in pure shock, looking at the green magic bouncing around his skin before he looks up at Lacey, and then he turns to me. Our eyes meet, and silently I try to tell him it's okay.

Even when it feels like a storm has just started in my chest and that storm is going to take every bit of hope from me.

Daniel doesn't move for a long time, and Lacey follows his gaze back to me, her eyes narrowing as I quickly look away and back to the water. Out of the corner of my eye, I see Lacey walk to Daniel, and he places his hand on her back, leading her away from the crowd and towards the pathway to the crowds of people waiting at the top of the cliff to celebrate with them. To cheer about their mating.

And now it's my turn.

Everything is silent, even the violent sea and snow-filled sky seem to still for this moment as I take a step forward and my foot sinks into the warm water. It instantly glows green, so bright it hurts my eyes, and pulls me in, my body almost betraying my fear-filled mind as I sink into the water until my head falls under. The green light becomes blinding as I float in the water, seeing nothing but light, until a voice fills my mind.

"You are my chosen, Irin. My chosen."

Something appears in my hand as I'm pushed up to the surface, and I gasp as I rise out of the water on the other side, almost stumbling to my feet on the sand, seeing the green magic swirling around my body in thick waves. It bounces, almost violently, in swirls and waves before pulling away from me into a giant ball of green magic, much bigger than anyone else's.

Why the hell do I have to stand out in this of all things? With so many people watching? I can't bear to look or hear anyone as I watch the sphere of magic spin in the air before shooting across the sand right into the man in the middle of the pack.

A man of my nightmares.

A man who took my innocence, crushed it, and made me fear him.

The alpha of my pack.

CHAPTER
FOUR

)) ● ((

The silence is damning. Damning and hollow as I stare into the unfeeling hazel eyes of the wolf shifter who is apparently my fated mate. An alpha doesn't share his mate, so this is the only man in the entire world who the moon goddess believes I should be with. And he is a monster. The alpha doesn't move as green magic crackles around his body, picking up his fur cloak that hangs off his large shoulders. Thick black hair falls to his shoulders in a straight line, not a strand out of place, and his stern face is stoic as he looks at me. Water drips down my dress, my wet hair sticking to my shoulders, and all the warmth from the water is gone now. The magic is gone, replaced only with fear for what happens next.

"No."

His single word rings out across the beach to me, the few yards that are between us are like nothing. No. No to the mating? No, it being me the moon goddess chose as the alpha's mate?

I agree with him...hell no. Mating with this excuse of an alpha, a man with no soul and a scar on his chin I caused when I was fifteen, is a life I would rather not live. Only once have I ever thought about giving up on my life, once on a wintry day like this, caused by the same man I'm looking at right now. This is the second time I have wanted to give up completely.

Whispers and gasps from the crowd of wolves behind him and from the crowds on the cliff finally reach my ears, and I try to block out what they are saying even when some of their words are perfectly heard.

"Her? The alpha's mate? Disgusting!"

"Maybe the moon goddess made a terrible mistake."

"He should kill her and be done with it."

The whispers never stop, and the same thing is chanted as the alpha's eyes bleed from hazel to green, his wolf taking over. Then he takes one step forward towards me, and I itch to run, to turn and leave as fast as I can, but something tells me not to.

Maybe that bit of stubborn pride I have left. Mike always said pride is a bigger killer than any man. I can see his point as my legs refuse to move and I stay still as a deer caught in a wolf's gaze. The alpha walks right up to me, his closeness making me feel sick to my stomach as he grabs my throat and lifts me slightly off the ground. Not enough to strangle me or cut my airways off, but enough to make me gasp, to make me want to struggle. I claw at his arm to get him off, but I'm nothing but a fly buzzing around a cake to him. I can see it in his eyes, his eyes owned by his wolf.

"How did you trick the moon goddess herself into believing a rat like you could ever be an alpha's mate?" he demands, and when I don't answer, he shakes me harshly, tightening his grip for a second. A second enough for me to scream and gasp, coughing on air when he loosens his grip. He shakes his head, his eyes bleeding from green back to hazel. To think I once trusted those hazel eyes, I dreamt about them, I thought he was my real friend.

"I asked you a question, Irin."

"My name is Mairin to you, not Irin. M-my friends call me Irin, Alpha Sylvester Ravensword.

Kill me if you're going to do it. I have feared you for so long that you killing me is nothing more than the goddess giving me my wish."

The lie falls from my tongue easily, even if his name does not. The moon goddess never gave me my real wish, my wish I begged her for once, to kill him, the alpha's son, Sylvester Ravensword. Instead, in some twisted version of fate, she made him alpha and me his mate he has waited for. His eyes stay hazel, but in the corners I see the green struggling to take over. He slowly tightens his grip around my neck, and I close my eyes, wanting to see nothing in these last moments. I gasp as I struggle to breathe, instinctively smacking and scratching at his one hand holding me up by the neck. Fear and panic take over, making my eyes pop open just as I'm thrown across the sand. With a slam, I hit the hard sand on my side, and a cracking noise in my arm is followed by incredible pain as I scream.

"Irin!" I hear Daniel shout in the distance, a wolfy and deep noise just before a foot slams into my stomach once. Then twice, then again and again. The pain almost becomes numb when my voice gives out, and the kicks finally stop as I roll onto my back, looking up at Alpha Sylvester as he angrily kicks me one more time before stepping back, rubbing his hands over his face repeatedly.

"No one follows us. If anyone does, I will rip them to shreds," I hear Alpha Sylvester demand, and the noise of wolves fighting nearby mixes with the sound of the waves. A hand digs into my hair and pulls me up as I taste blood in my mouth. Everything is blurry as someone drags me by my hair and arm over sharp rocks that cut into my back and catch on my dress, but part of me detaches from my body, drifting into a world of no pain as I fade in and out of consciousness. Eventually I'm dropped onto grass, and I blink my eyes a few times, coughing on the blood in my mouth and turning my head to the side, every inch of my body hurting so badly the pain threatens to knock me out with every breath. A hand wraps around my throat once more, and I'm lifted into the air, my feet hanging as I struggle to breathe.

"Open your eyes," Alpha Sylvester demands, his fiery breath blowing across my face.

Opening my eyes is harder than I thought it would be, and when I do, I see he is right in front of me.

"I can't kill you, because my wolf will not allow it." He shakes me once. "Die in the sea for your fated mate, Irin. Die like you should have so many years ago, because if the sea does not take you, I will know. I will know, and I will never stop sending wolves to kill you. I have rejected you as my mate, you are not worthy of me, and you never could be. You are nothing."

"Then why does the moon goddess think otherwise?" I whisper back with all the strength I have. I should plead for my life, I should beg and cry, but I just stare at him as his eyes flash with pure anger, and he roars as he lets me go. The wind cannot catch my body as I fly off the cliff, well aware the sea is going to take my life in seconds.

And in those seconds I fall, I still pray to the moon goddess for someone to catch me.

CHAPTER
FIVE

))●((

"Get the healer ready!" a deep voice demands, nothing more than a groggy sound to my sore ears as I struggle to wake up. Coldness like I've never known controls my body from head to toe, and it's not just cold, I'm soaking wet too. Every inch of my body hurts. Even my eyelids ache as I pull them open to see rocks in front of me. Smooth white rocks. Waves crash in the distance, and I can smell nothing but damp water. Lifting my head, which takes more strength than I thought it would, I see I'm still in my mating ceremony dress, but it's ripped around my stomach, and a large cut snakes down my ribs, hidden under the ripped fabric of my dress. My bare feet are stuck in the wet sand, and I'm curled up in a space between a group of rocks like the sea threw me here.

Flashes of memories attack me quickly. The sea. The mating ceremony. The alpha who was meant to be my mate but instead tried to kill me... How am I alive?

Scuffling of heavy booted feet reminds me I'm not alone, and I jump away from the noise behind me, pivoting to see a man standing on the rock. His silhouette blocks out the light, making all around him glow as I drift my eyes up his body. Thick black trousers cover large thighs, and he has a black shirt tucked into them. The shirt stretches across his large shoulders, large enough to make him a champ at a rugby match if he chose it. Following my eyes up over his golden skin, I suck in a deep breath when I see his face.

He is beautiful in a way men shouldn't be allowed to be. Strong jawline, high cheekbones, perfectly shaped lips and thick black eyelashes that surround clear blue eyes that remind me of a lake— still, in an eerie way that makes you wonder if there is any life below the waters. Black locks of hair that are a little too long, falling just over his eyes when the wind blows, look softer than the silk dress I'm wearing.

No one in my pack ever looked like him. I would have noticed.

The more I stare, the longer I realise he is staring right back at me, like he has seen a ghost. Like I'm familiar to him. Considering where I came from, he might have done. Not that I have a clue where we are. I lean up on my one arm, but I can't see out of the rocks or anything around the man standing over me.

Correction: the wolf. He is watching me like a wolf, that I am certain of. He is too direct, too inhuman like, and all that I need to see now is his eyes glow.

"Do you know me?" I ask, my voice throaty, and I clear it, tasting nothing but thick salt left over from the sea.

The man tilts his head to the side. "Why are you here?"

"I-I was..." I pause because I have no idea where I am, and telling this wolf I'm the alpha's rejected mate might not be the best idea if I'm still in Ravensword lands. He will drag me back to the alpha, who will try to kill me again. No, I can't do that.

"Answer me."

The man's command is clear, ringing with

power and frustration. I look up, meeting his eyes once more even when I can't think straight or of a single word to say. Whatever I say is going to get me killed, and I can't help but think I've been given a second chance at life. I should never have survived falling into the sea, not with the injuries I have, not when I passed out, but here I am. Alive.

It's clear the moon goddess has much more planned for me than I know.

When I don't say a word for a long time, he moves. The man moves so quickly, and within seconds he is in my face, leaning over me on the rocks. His nose gently touches mine, my body a mix with fear and curiosity.

"Tell me," he commands once more. "Tell me why you are on the shores of the Fall Mountain Pack, or you will die this very second."

Fall Mountain Pack?

Oh my god... How am I alive and on this island? I know people usually die who try to swim between the islands, but for me to have gotten here unconscious is nothing short of magic. I'm yet to decide what kind of magic, considering all I know about the Fall Mountain Pack is that they are cruel and vicious. That they live in ways most wolves would never do or even think about. They don't trade with the Ravensword Pack, and every attempt at peace has been met with death. We are told they are monsters, and now I'm on their lands.

But truthfully, I'm dead either way. If they send me back, the alpha will kill me, and if I stay here, it's likely they will kill me.

I have nothing to lose by telling this man the truth.

"My name is Mairin Perdita, and I am a rejected mate of the Ravensword Pack," I announce, leaning back against the rocks and curling my legs underneath myself, needing space from his man. His eyes widen, but he doesn't say a word. "The mating ceremony named me as the alpha's mate, and because I am a foster child with no family or worth, he rejected me. After hurting me in anger, he tried to kill me by throwing me off a cliff. How I'm here, alive, is a mystery to me, but I guess I am asking for your help. I'm asking for a damn miracle, because my life has been anything but one."

"I would wager surviving your rejection is a miracle. The sea is a cruel mistress at the best of times, and last night was one of the worst storms seen in years," he finally replies, leaning back, his voice less hostile than it was. "I can always tell when someone is lying to me, and you are not, Mairin Perdita. My name is Alpha Henderson Fall, and I am going to help you."

"You're the alpha?" I whisper in shock and a little fear. It shouldn't surprise me he is so high in rank, just because of how commanding and powerful he comes across as, but it does.

"One of the four," he answers and moves closer. "You are weak, my wolf senses it, and I must carry you. Will you allow me? It is a twenty-minute walk to the lighthouse where there is a healer."

The part of me that hates being touched, especially by men, makes me want to say no and stubbornly try to climb out of these rocks myself. But I know I can't. Every inch of me hurts, my stomach is bleeding, and my ankle looks swollen. Somehow I have survived the sea, but without help, I will not survive much longer. I nod once, unable to actually agree, and I'm sure my hesitancy shines in my eyes as he comes closer and wraps his arms underneath me before effortlessly picking me up. In order to steady myself, my hands go out around his neck, brushing against a necklace there that is tucked into his shirt. Henderson jumps out of the rocks, and I look around me to see a tall mountain right in front of us, and a small forest lies between the beach and the mountain. The mountain is topped with snow, and several caves look like they have lights inside from this distance. The beach is long with rocky sand and harsh waves that crash against everything they hit, and in the distance, I see a faded blue lighthouse with its bright light turning in circles. Henderson is silent as he jumps off the rocks into the sand and eats up the space between us and the lighthouse with his enormous steps. After a few minutes, I relax my shoulders a little.

"Is it just luck you found me, or do you live around here?" I question.

Henderson looks down at me, his blue eyes hard to read. "What do you know of my pack, Mairin?"

"That you are monsters," I tell him, remembering well how he said he could sense if I was lying.

His lips tilt up into a dazzling smile. "Lies are so easily told to those who live in fear, and your alpha lied, Mairin. We were never the monsters, but our life differs greatly from where you have come from. Here we don't have fated mates, we only mate with who we fall in love with. Wolves are free to date, to explore, to do whatever they want, and the only new wolves we accept into the pack are rejected or lost.

We respect loyalty, and we take in those who are nothing to others."

"There have been other rejected mates?" I ask.

His smile falls. "I collect over one wolf a week from this shore. All of them rejected and thrown into the sea because their mate could not convince their wolf to kill them."

"I had no idea," I whisper.

"To answer your question," Henderson states, shifting me a little in his arms, "I do not live here, but I am called to the lighthouse every day to check out who has arrived. If you had lied to me, or if you were someone who just escaped the pack, then I am tasked with ending your life. We do not take in those who desert their pack and family. We want only those who will be loyal."

My heart beats fast in my chest, hearing the sincerity of his voice. He would have killed me. "So you kill for loyalty?"

"No, I kill for my pack," he answers, his tone clarifying that is the last of our conversation, and I rest back, watching the sea and the very outline of the land in the distance, hidden by clouds. All I can think of is Daniel and Jesper, and even Mike. I have to hope they look after each other, because I can't ever go back.

The Ravensword alpha is my mate, and he will do worse than reject me next time, he will have someone kill me.

So I have to make the Fall Mountain Pack my new home, whatever it takes.